The Music of What Happens

The Purple House Anthology of New Writing

Edited by Tanya Farrelly

NEW ISLAND

THE MUSIC OF WHAT HAPPENS
First published in 2020 by
New Island Books
Glenshesk House
10 Richview Office Park
Clonskeagh
Dublin 14, D14 V8C4
Republic of Ireland
www.newisland.ie

Print ISBN: 978-1-84840-776-3
eBook ISBN: 978-1-84840-777-0

Typeset by JVR Creative, India
Copy-edited by Djinn von Noorden
Cover design by Fiachra McCarthy, fiachramccarthy.com
Printed by ScandBook, Sweden

New Island Books is a member of Publishing Ireland.

Contents

Foreword

Welcome to *The Music of What Happens*. The idea to publish an anthology of this nature came about when we were discussing how we could celebrate our thirty years of Purple House Cancer Support in the community.

I was inspired to set up a cancer support centre following my own experience of cancer when I was in my early twenties. My aim was to provide emotional support and practical help to people whose lives had been affected by the illness. At the time there was little or no emotional support for a person living with a cancer diagnosis and while the medical side was well covered within the medical profession, the concept of a cancer support group was somewhat alien in Ireland in 1990.

So around my kitchen table in February of that year, my husband Brendan and I set about building the first community-based cancer support centre of its kind in Ireland. Our vision was very clear: we wanted to create a warm and welcoming environment where people could come together and be sure of a sympathetic listening ear, no matter what their social, economic or cultural background. We felt at that time that if our experience could help others, even one family, then what we had suffered would have been worthwhile.

Within a week of telling my story to the local media, I was contacted by seven individuals who felt, as I did, that a cancer support centre was needed in the community.

In the words of Kevin Costner in *Field of Dreams*, that if you build it, they will come – build it we did, and they came in their hundreds within the first few years.

We were initially offered a room free of charge in the local parish centre. This enabled us to hold meetings and invite guest speakers to talk about various topics such as stress management, coping skills, family relationships and so on. Before long, phone calls to my home were coming in thick and fast and very soon it became clear that we needed to rent our own premises with our own phone line; a place where we could provide a private room for counselling and telephone support. We secured a small rented space in Carlton Terrace, off Main Street in Bray, where we remained for three years. It wasn't ideal, but it was a base and it provided privacy for those who needed it. Soon it became more widely known that there was a cancer support centre in Bray. People travelled locally, from Arklow, Tallaght and Roundwood, with phone calls for help and support from as far away as Sligo and Donegal.

In time it became apparent that more specific services were needed. I was asked to do a house call to a young woman who had been diagnosed with breast cancer. She had three young children and her most pressing worry at the time was her youngest child. He was having difficulty with his speech and they didn't know where to go for help and so I became an avenue of communication between the various health agencies, especially when the family, for one reason or another, were unable to do so themselves.

We became a registered charity in 1998 shortly before President Mary MacAleese came and officially opened our cancer support centre. She later contacted us again when we celebrated our twentieth anniversary and invited a group of us into Áras an Uachtaráin for afternoon tea and a tour. Becoming a registered charity enabled us to apply for grants to run various courses and groups and this in turn helped us to reach a wider audience.

Our profile had been raised considerably by President MacAleese's opening of our drop-in centre on Bray Main Street. But we could no longer manage on volunteer commitment alone so nine years into the life of Purple House, I entered into negotiations with the HSE to secure a grant to pay a part-time counsellor and a part-time receptionist so we could ensure that our doors remained open every day. We were awarded a small annual grant, which was a major boost to us. Other sources of funding included project-based grants from the Community Foundation for Ireland, the National Programme for Age and Opportunity, a grant from the Department of Health for bereavement counselling and grants from Wicklow County Council and Dun Laoghaire County Council. Statutory funding only accounted for approximately one quarter of our overall funding, so voluntary fundraising continued to take place in order for us to keep providing our services free of charge.

We were also contacted by people from all across Ireland who wanted to set up similar groups in their own county: as a result, we travelled the length and breadth of Ireland giving talks and presentations on how to set up a community-based cancer support centre.

We became increasingly integrated with other health-related agencies. HSE referrals flooded in from hospitals and clinics, as did self-referrals. The numbers using our services continue to grow year on year. Purple House now provides psycho-oncology and psychosocial support to over 1,500 families every year.

I was invited onto the patient forum for the last National Cancer Strategy and advocated strongly for a community-based cancer support system in Ireland. As a member of the HSE consultative committee for palliative care in Wicklow, I campaigned strongly for palliative and end-of-life care for those people wishing to remain in their own homes. There are more people living with cancer in the world today than at any other time and nobody should suffer in isolation and alone.

The increased demand on our services here in Purple House is a vindication of what I sought to achieve in 1990. Today Purple House has developed into a nationwide charity, supporting cancer patients across Ireland. This would not have been possible without the commitment and support of all those around me: my family, my friends and the many wonderful people who have come through the doors of Purple House, some of whom are sadly no longer with us. Special thanks in particular to the community, for they embraced my vision from the very start and have continued to support us throughout the past thirty years.

Back in 1998, as a young mother of two boys, mine was perhaps a unique story, but today there are many more like me. I am so grateful that I followed my heart and pushed against the odds to ensure that Purple House is a place within our community, for our community, and will be here for many more years to come.

Thank you.

Veronica O'Leary
Founder and Director of Services
Purple House Cancer Support

Editor's Note

Tanya Farrelly

I first came into contact with Purple House in my role as director of Bray Literary Festival. It had occurred to me that while hosting the festival, we could also use the opportunity to raise money for a local charity. And so began my research.

In April 2015 we lost my beautiful mother, Patsy, to multiple myeloma – a cancer of the blood that affects the white cells made in the bone marrow. We had already lost my sister-in-law, Joan, that January, to the same illness. She was fifty-four. My best friend's mother had passed away from multiple myeloma in 2010. A lady in my writing group was diagnosed with it and another friend's mother, having died from heart trouble, was discovered posthumously to have had the disease: and yet research showed that this was a rare type of cancer mostly found in African males. The cause is currently unknown, but there are links between its manifestation and the use of chemicals, with car mechanics, hairdressers and agricultural workers said to be most at risk. According to the Irish Cancer Society there are currently around two thousand people living with multiple myeloma in Ireland.

When I discovered Purple House, I knew that it was the charity I wanted to become involved with. Here was an organisation set up to offer free counselling, complementary therapies and recreational classes to survivors of and those still suffering from cancer, along with their family members. I contacted the charity and had a meeting with Conor and Stephanie, telling them about my idea to raise money for the organisation at the festival, and also about my own experience of losing my mother. During that meeting I mentioned that I would like very much to offer my skills as a creative writing facilitator if this was something that would interest those who availed of their services.

The Friday that the festival was to begin, I drove up to Purple House to pick up their collection buckets – alas, I didn't know that they only worked a half-day on Fridays! Determined to keep my promise, I went online and printed off the Purple House logo, which I attached to a cardboard box with sticky tape. Then I announced that we were raising money for this wonderful and much-needed charity. The box looked dodgy as hell, but people saw the funny side and gave generously. Indeed, over that weekend we raised €500 thanks to the writers and festival-goers, many of whom had been affected by cancer or the loss of loved ones themselves.

Last year Veronica contacted me to ask if I would teach a ten-week course, the first of three ten-week blocks I would go on to facilitate at Purple House. At first the group was tentative – what could they expect from a class entitled 'Empowerment through Writing'? We established that many people were interested in writing personal essays while others were keen to try their hand at fiction. Soon everyone was sharing their stories and I am delighted to include a selection of participants' work in this anthology.

It was Veronica's idea to publish a book as part of the thirtieth anniversary celebrations for Purple House. She didn't have to convince me to come on board. As soon as I got home that evening I began contacting writers I admired to tell them about the project and ask if they would be willing to contribute a piece. The positive response was overwhelming.

Writers asked if there was a theme for the anthology. We decided that the best thing would be not to restrict subject matter. This is not a book about cancer, but rather a celebration of the endeavours of Purple House and those who come through its doors. Themes that have emerged from the many stories, poems and essays that follow include music, friendship, knowledge, childhood, ageing, love, bereavement, displacement and survival; the themes of everyday life and how we live it. I have attempted to organise the work according to these themes, twinning each poem with a companion piece of prose. This, surprisingly, came about quite organically.

I am honoured to have been involved in this project and to present you, the reader, with an eclectic array of voices, both new and professional. I would like to thank Purple House for the opportunity to collaborate, and the writers who have given so selflessly to make this the wonderful book that it is.

A Friday Night in January

Anne Tannam

When you head out, expecting nothing
from the night; cycle to a charity gig
you'd reluctantly promised to go to
and finding a place to lock the bike
on the square outside
you walk down basement stairs,
the muffled thrum of music, urgent and pulsing,
pushing you through doors into
a teeming crowd swaying in their seats,
buzzing around the bar, sparking off the energy
coming from the low stage
where five members of a middle-aged band
are playing like it's the Last Waltz;
like it's their last dance before
the clock strikes twelve
and before you know it
you've stepped off the edge,
stepped into the mystery
of what it means to be in Dublin
in a basement bar, on a Friday night in January
and much, much later, when you re-emerge
a soft rain is falling on the square, on your bike,
on the swans resting on the canal bank;
and on the final stretch of hushed road

an unexpected encore:
a fox appears on the footpath ahead,
crosses the road in front of you,
the music of her movements a song –
in the back of your throat –
before disappearing
through a garden gate
to silent, rapturous applause.

Dress Code

Anne Marie Byrne

'So, what's on the agenda for this evening?' asked Pete, the record producer.

We were in my friend Liz's Earl's Court flat. It was back in the late seventies and I had called to visit my friend on my day off thinking we might do something for the afternoon or evening.

'I don't know,' Liz replied to her boyfriend with an air of indifference. 'I'm not sure I want to do anything in particular. I have work early in the morning and I feel quite tired.'

'There's a film on in the Screen on the Green in Islington that I'd like to go to,' I said, 'it's called *The Missouri Breaks.*'

'Oh, I've heard of that,' said Liz, 'the reviews were good. It's a western, isn't it?'

'Yes, that's right,' I said. 'I missed it when it came out a few months ago. It sounds really good, with Marlon Brando and Jack Nicholson. They're just showing it for one night in the Green, so I definitely want to go tonight.'

Liz uttered a sound that was a mixture of a moan and a sigh, saying that she heard there was a lot of violence and cruelty in the film and didn't think it would appeal to her.

'Well it *is* a western,' I said, 'and it is about the conflict between a rancher and a farmer with a bounty hunter thrown in for good measure, so I'd say the possibility of violence and cruelty is fairly high.'

'Not for me, not tonight,' said Liz in a tone that made it clear she was not for turning.

'How about you, Pete?' I asked. 'Do you fancy a night at the cinema?'

'I'm afraid it's not for me either,' he answered. 'I'm working this evening, so I'll leave you ladies to decide what you want to do.' Then he added conspiratorially: 'But here's an exclusive I'll let you in on – The Sex Pistols are playing a late-night gig tonight after the film is over … it's a secret gig.'

'Are you serious? Are you sure? Are you going? Can you get me a ticket?' Pete's announcement had fired me up and I couldn't contain my excitement at the prospect of getting to see the most controversial band of the time. The Sex Pistols had been banned from public appearances as a result of what were perceived to be their anarchic tendencies. Notwithstanding their political leanings they were also rude, unpredictable and edgy. There was a strong possibility that violence would erupt at their gigs, especially since Sid Vicious had replaced Glen Matlock as bass player in the line-up. Pete said no, he wouldn't be going himself and he didn't have any free tickets.

'It's a secret gig,' he said, 'it's just for people who're invited, people in the know.'

'Well, I'm in the know now,' I said, 'so how do I get in?'

'You can take your chances in the queue. They'll probably let in some token members of the public so they won't be accused of elitism or exclusivity. Or if you really want to be there and you're going to the cinema anyway you could hide in the auditorium after the film and just infiltrate the gig if you have the guts to do it.'

Seeing as Pete had arrived at Liz's flat about ten minutes after me, I felt that maybe it would be best to leave the two of them alone, especially as he was working that night and she was on duty early in the morning. So I made my exit and set out to walk to my own little bedsit in Shepherd's Bush. I was a fit and healthy twenty-year-old and quite the flâneur (should that be flâneuse?) back then so I thought nothing of walking miles around the London boroughs despite the variety of public transport that was available. Walking kept me grounded and also allowed me to get a really good overview of the layout of London. In this instance it gave me a chance to formulate my thoughts on the night ahead. As is so often the case when your best friend is in a relationship and you are not, I was used to being left to my own resources when it came to going out for entertainment. In my enforced state of independence, the prospect of going to the cinema on my own didn't faze me in the least. However, the thought of trying to wangle my way into the most notorious gig of the year so far was a preoccupation that kept me engrossed for the duration of the two-mile journey home.

The Missouri Breaks was a good film: it did contain violence and cruelty, as Liz had predicted, but it was a level of violence and cruelty that I could easily tolerate back then. On that night in the Screen on the Green, the cinema was half full and there was no indication that anyone in the audience had any idea what was about to unfold in its midst by the time they made it back to their homes or to the pub. When the final credits rolled, I headed for the ladies' loo. I got myself into a cubicle and settled in for the long wait. Luckily, I'd brought a paperback to pass the time in those pre-mobile days. With my complete belief in Pete's insider knowledge, it never occurred to me that at some stage I might be plunged into complete darkness and locked in an empty cinema overnight. After about an hour, voices began to become audible outside the door of my cubicle and I eventually plucked up the courage to emerge. The auditorium was filling up by the time I drifted out to take my place. The scene was utterly different to when I had left it an hour earlier.

I was quite overwhelmed by the assault on my senses. It was like I had entered a parallel universe. Punks of every shape and size filled the stalls. Piercings, pins and spikes were in abundance, black was the dominant colour, lightened by the occasional patch of tartan. Men and women wore make-up, mainly of a very pale hue, with eyes and lips emphasised by ghoulish black or purple. The air was heavy with the smoke of cigarettes and joints and electric with the air of expectation.

The gig itself was as exciting as I had anticipated. Initially we were treated to what seemed like home movies of the Sex Pistols posing and performing around London: this was an early project of Julien Temple, who subsequently became a film and music-video director and renowned chronicler of the punk era.

Next on the programme was a set from The Slits. They were a group who went on to garner some notoriety as the only all-female punk group who managed to get their act together, who could play their instruments and write witty lyrics. However, on this occasion they were raw teenagers, undisciplined and prone to unruly interactions on stage. Nevertheless, it was exciting to see them at this embryonic stage when they exuded unfettered possibility. Looking back now it's somewhat disappointing to realise that they never really achieved their true potential as the forebears of girl power.

It must have been two o'clock before the main act hit the stage. Despite the build-up of anticipation, the opening number turned out to be a damp squib, coming to a halt shortly after it began due to lack of cohesion among the group members. Finally, after some fumbling and bickering, the show got going again and this time continued right through most of the songs from the *Never Mind the Bollocks* album. Although the exhilaration was palpable in the audience it didn't seem to be transmitting to Johnny Rotten on stage as he continually rebuked the audience and urged them to 'wake up'. Sid Vicious (who had made his debut in the Pistols a few weeks previously at a short gig in the Notre Dame Hall off Leicester Square in London's West End) had seemingly learned the basics of bass-playing in the meantime but for the most part chose to spend his time berating the audience and indeed spitting on them. He had been chosen by Malcolm McLaren not for his musical ability but for his looks and his attitude. Nonetheless, the other members of the band, Steve Jones on guitar and Paul Cook on drums, managed to keep it together sufficiently to deliver a memorable performance. The musicians certainly tested the limits of their instruments and Malcolm McLaren on the sound desk contributed to the surreal effects with distortion and overload. Johnny Rotten on vocals snarled and sneered his way through the set, continuing to harangue the audience while gyrating around the stage. It struck me that for all his punk posing and posturing Rotten actually looked like he had borrowed many of his best swaggers and struts from none other than Mick Jagger, a decidedly mainstream performer by this time.

It was certainly a night to remember for many reasons, not least of which was my own discomfort in the surroundings. It wouldn't have bothered me so much if *I* wasn't the one who stood out in the crowd. Yes, in my carefully constructed plan of infiltration I had forgotten one thing – to blend in! In a sea of highly quaffed, heavily made-up youth I looked like I had just wandered in from a folk music festival. My long wavy hair was *au naturel*, as was my bare, scrubbed face. Most excruciating of all was that my outfit left a lot to be desired in terms of punk credibility. In fact, my flower-print pinafore dress would have looked more at home in a Laura Ashley shop window than at a punk rock gig.

So for me the night of one of the most outrageous gigs of the seventies was in some ways like having an out-of-body experience. I was there but I wasn't fully present. I was a witness but not a participant. On the inside I was fully tuned in to my surroundings, enjoying the music and the mayhem, yet at the same time I was aware that on the outside I looked utterly out of place due to my own negligence in failing to consider the dress code.

The Great Friend
(from *about:blank*)

Adam Wyeth

In the autumn of 1244

a young Muslim scholar of Konya
met a new arrival who'd been travelling

throughout the Middle East.

This stranger put a question to the scholar:
it remains one of the great mysteries.

Whatever the question,

the young scholar lost his breath and fainted.
When he came round the two talked and became

locked in a stream of endless dialogue.

Inseparable, they spoke for days without human need –
like two musicians riffing, each one taking over where

the other left off in a state of pure discovery.

Late one night, mid-discussion,
the friend went to attend a knock at the door

and didn't come back.

The young scholar fell silent and vowed never
to speak again unless his great friend returned.

He had fallen into what is known

as the deep well of meditation, the narrow
tunnel of mortal contemplation.

For months, not a word passed his lips.

Then on his darkest night he looked up
and let out a savage howl. As he screamed

he found a new voice forming.

The next morning, he headed to the market square
and began to speak. Poetry and parables poured out:

You are the sky my spirit circles in.

My soul is from elsewhere. He started
to sway and outstretching his arms whirled around,

spinning between food stalls,

weaving parables out of chickpeas; forming fables
about burnt kebabs. A large crowd gathered,

some started to swoon and dissolve

into laughter, others moaned in ecstasy
and cried. One young man began writing

his every word down.

The Konya scholar had lost all simile
and became the thing itself: the lover, the beggar,

the parched earth, the unfurling flower.

He continued turning into the small hours,
his great friend returning through him.

A mute moon smiling in the wings.

The Black Eye

David Butler

How I got it?

At Dun Laoghaire, a family group of North American ruminants boarded, encroached, sat and expanded laterally. By Monkstown they'd begun to creak at each other like animate sofas. That put paid to today's *Crosaire*.

'*Crass*-word, huh?' the adult female beamed over half-moon bifocals. Talkers. Of course they were. Atop a gargantuan neck, the adult male's inflamed features mock-grimaced. Indolent as Buddhas, the pair of offspring looked on.

I returned the female a watery smile, knitted my brows, resumed the newspaper. 8 down still eluded. So too 11 down, and 22 across, a little taunting bastard that should by rights have been 'inch'. But 'inch' couldn't be made to square with 20 down, 'assegai'. And 'assegai' was a banker. Three times I tried to reread the clue. Three times I failed. Words cavorted like three-year-olds aware they were being indulgently watched. Ever since Monkstown my thumb had been clicking out a warning Morse on my Parker, which Mother Hubbard chose to ignore.

'Tough, huh?'

I laid down the pen. OK, lady. While I calculated I twitched the paper in intimation of consulting it. Then I cleared my throat. 'Supersize honours headless conurbation.'

'*Scuse* me?'

'Seven letters,' I prompted.

Faces, huge as balloons, blinked variously.

'Blank-B-blank-blank-I-blank-Y?'

The blimps bobbled blankly, side to side.

'I dunno how *any*one's supposed to figure those,' groaned the elder offspring. College-age, so far as one could tell. She appeared to be some sort of authority among them. I lifted the paper and frowned instead at the chess puzzle, Portisch versus Gligoric, black to play and mate. But concentration was quite hopeless. Above the fold the adult male narrowed his eyes and nodded slowly at me in what might have been intended as *I know when I'm being joshed, my friend.*

Now *that* I doubted.

After about a fortnight the train sashayed into Tara Street. Lightly, I alighted with a jaunty wave towards my American buddies, not quite minding the gap.

Outside, the immediate problem was what to do with the newspaper. The twenty-eight minutes from Dalkey to Tara Street were all I ever allowed the cryptic. But today's grid was still marred by a half-dozen gaps, and one long entry that ill-fitted like one of those celibate jigsaw pieces coerced into obdurate coupling. Abandon it? Or slide it into a side pocket for a sneaky look later? The second option I might have adopted without a second thought, except for the consideration that I was meeting Sabrina for lunch, and things with Sabrina were not going well.

Sabrina Dziczek could never see why I bothered with crosswords. A waste of time, she called them. So too *Only Connect* and *University Challenge*. So too the correspondence chess, which advanced at a glacial pace on one corner of the kitchen table. She failed to understand my visceral abhorrence at the proliferation of apostrophes in shop signs, an indifference I failed to understand given that she worked as an EFL teacher. Apropos, there's a story I imparted to her of Stephen Joyce refusing a copyright request by means of an indignant telegram, which declared: '*Finnegans Wake does not have an apostrophe in it's title.*' She simply would not appreciate the delicious perfection of that impish possessive.

She'd arranged for us to lunch in an Italian off Parliament Street. It was to be an act of contrition on my part. I've no time for what they call social media, so had not been prompted by Facebook that yesterday was her birthday: not that Facebook would have alerted me that it was what they term a 'significant' birthday, since she never confided her age to any public profile that I was aware of. My antennae might have picked up the white noise of her terseness the previous evening had I not been immersed in a rerun of Simon Schama on BBC4. It did eventually register that she was touching up her make-up in the hall. When a featureless voice announced she was 'going on a girls' night out', my faux pas came to me. 'Yes,' she forestalled, gurning into her compact and snapping it shut. 'Perhaps if you were as interested in birthdays as you are in the dates of English battles ...'

English battles. She was no dummy, Sabrina.

The train had arrived fifteen minutes late, due, as the PA helpfully explained, to 'operational reasons'. I was already running late. And of course, the café, or more correctly the trattoria, was nowhere to be found. Frantically I scanned the signage above either footpath – Parliament Street isn't particularly long. But of Vesuvius, neither hide nor hair was to be seen. I considered using Google maps. I was still only eight minutes behind schedule. But something stayed my hand.

I returned to an unlikely door. Stuck to its window, on what looked like a cheap transfer, were: the outline of a volcanic peak; the word *Trattoria*; a dog-leg arrow; the figure 50m. Vesuvius was not, in fact, on Parliament Street. It was *off* Parliament Street. But I was already on the back foot. To bring up the inaccuracy in her directions was unlikely to thaw the Polish winter in Sabrina Dziczek.

She was sitting in a corner by the window. In fact, I clocked her red anorak before I clocked her. I waved cheerily from the hatstand, was drawn forward in the tractor beam of her gaze, and made my vague excuses as I sat.

'I've already ordered,' she declared, looking away.

Now that I was sitting, the newspaper poked up out of the pocket of my sports jacket, so I took it out and laid it on the table. Big mistake. The incomplete crossword was face up, cheekily implying that I intended to run my eye over it. Those goddamned Americans! Hurriedly, belatedly, I flipped it over. My apologetic smirk went unacknowledged. Then I unthinkingly opened the menu. The first category I lighted on was *Pizza's*. I coughed. *Pizza's* was bad enough. But lurking in the next column, about halfway down, was *Panini's*. Now, *Paninis* on its own might have been tolerable. *Paninis* I might have coped with. But the double whammy of the double plural coupled with the burst-appendix punctuation made me stifle a guffaw. It did not go unnoticed.

I wasn't hungry in the slightest. I'm no great fan of Italian cuisine at the best of times. Probably, that's why Sabrina had picked the place. The vegetarian lasagne seemed the least worst option. With a glass of house red, what the hell. Merlot, I had little doubt. By the time the order arrived we were at least talking. Which is to say, Sabrina was talking.

The problem was, there was a party of three buckos over by the cashier's station, lounging boisterously underneath an antique map of the Bay of Naples. Rugby types. D4.

Up to this point I'd been able to block out their bluster and filter the import of what Sabrina was saying. But then one of them came out with 'Dude, I was being ironic.' When I'd lay odds that what he was being was sarcastic. Because irony, to my mind, implies a situation or circumstance. *Olympic Swimmer Drowns in Bathtub*. Now that would be ironic. Curiously, the *OED* appears to side with the rugby-heads on this one: 'irony, *n.*, 1 an expression of meaning, often humorous or sarcastic, by the use of language of a different or opposite tendency.' You'd think the *OED* would be above populist concessions.

Sabrina was staring straight at me. An interrogative stare, in which not a little bafflement was spangling. It declared, You haven't been listening to a word I've been saying, have you?

I recovered the most recent substantive. 'Transylvania. Go on.'

'What about Transylvania?'

'You've been looking up where we should stay.'

'Where we should stay *where?*'

'Brasov.' This was an educated guess. It achieved the bare minimum required.

'So?' Her eyes narrowed. 'Which place do you think?'

Time to risk all on the turn of a card. 'Whichever is most central, no? Be worth the extra few bucks. I mean, how often do you go on a honeymoon?' Rhetorical. Then the master play. 'You?'

Equilibrium restored, Sabrina lost herself in her disquisition as our respective lunches gave up their warmth to the ambient air. And all would have been fine if Ross O'Carroll Kelly hadn't kicked off again about five minutes in.

'No, you're all wrong guys: 2001, England beat us. I know for a *fact*, because my father, yah, had actually *betted* on them to win.'

Now this was patent bollocks. I knew for a *fact* that 2001 was the year of the foot-and-mouth. And the year of the foot-and-mouth we'd beaten England. The whole schedule had been thrown out of kilter. Half of the games had to be played in the autumn. And in 2001, Keith Wood had pulled off that wrap-around try off the line out. OK, we'd already blown the slam up in Murrayfield. But that victory had been oh so sweet …

There was the grind and shudder of chair legs being dragged back. Sabrina was on her feet. She crumpled a petulant napkin and dropped it on the table. Her anorak was hoisting up her back by the time she'd pushed out through the exit.

To follow an incensed fiancée out of a café isn't as straight-forward as you might think. First, there is the little matter of the bill to pay. With one eye on Sabrina Dziczek's disappearing red hood, I scanned the room. And, of course, that was precisely the juncture when no waitress was to be found. Helplessly I peered at her fork, abandoned in the entrails of her spaghetti arrabbiata as though she'd been searching for an omen there. Beside the newspaper, still cowering face down, the soggy brick of my vegetarian lasagne had begun to subside.

I abandoned table and guilty newspaper and hurried to the cashier's station, my haste registered if not remarked upon by the three wise men. I was hoping my urgency would somehow conjure the cashier. One of the trio, who bore a bizarre resemblance to Dick Spring, paused briefly before going on with his diatribe.

'I still say it was an inspired substitution on behalf of Joe Schmitt.'

Ignore! No time.

In the adjoining room a waitress orbited the stairwell and cleared a far table with a consummate avoidance of my eye. I could see the red anorak recede towards the cobbles of Temple Bar like something out of *Schindler's List*.

'Excuse me!' I called towards the empty space, which the waitress had fleetingly filled.

'*And*,' opined Ross O'Carroll Kelly, poking a finger towards Dick Spring, 'it was really tight post-match analysis on his behalf.'

'For Christ's sake!' I cried. They stared. 'It's on his part!'

'Sorry, dude? Are you talking to us?'

'It's on his part! It's not on his fucking *behalf*!'

Heavily, the three men stood, blocking my way to the exit. They were going to enjoy this.

The Ghosts Next Door

Edward O'Dwyer

They are at it again, the ghosts next door.
They are having loud, devil-may-care sex.

There is nobody living in the house next door.
An estate agent comes by from time to time,
some upkeep, straightening the sign out front.
The lights are always switched off in there.

We've tried banging on the walls, shouting out
for some quiet, but the ghosts ignore us.

We are talking about bills that need paying,
and how the kids aren't doing so well at school,
and how the dog's infection has come back,

and they are making love, all their moans
high and haunting. She died first, he followed
three months later. Those were three months

of silence, as though he was just waiting,
as though he was just sitting and waiting.

Immediately after, it began, the sex.
Every night we hear them at it. Insatiable.

We don't have sex anymore, with neither
the time nor the energy. We are too worried,
frustrated, anxious, regretful. We are insecure.
Instead we try to get some sleep before work.

We lay in our bed, our bodies separated,
and we listen to the ghosts next door,
and we wonder how living has come to this.

The Entrancement

Rosemary Jenkinson

One morning I was sitting in my office, leafing through some manuscripts, when there was a knock on my door.

A Japanese man let himself into the room without waiting for an answer. He was a strange-looking character with a shaven head, a pale, cadaverous face and dark, loose linen clothes that hung so limply they might have been on a washing line.

'Sorry,' said Grace, my assistant editor, following behind him. 'He wouldn't wait.'

'That's OK, Grace,' I said, nodding for her to leave us. I didn't feel the man was any threat. Though he was shockingly thin, he was quiet-eyed and his lightly-hunched shoulders suggested shyness. 'What can I do for you?'

'Your magazine includes ghost stories, doesn't it?' he asked in a soft Japanese accent. He spoke formally, like a serious student of English. It was like he'd stepped straight out of the nineteenth century.

'Mysteries, horror, the generally dark and arcane. You name it.'

'Do you write yourself?'

'From time to time. When I get a break from editing.'

'I was wondering if you'd be interested in hearing a story, one that's affected me directly. Perhaps later you can write it down, let the world know about it because it's all true.'

The writer in me jumped at the chance, though my more rational side had misgivings. The point was, my passion lay in the fictional, in the world of the imagination. It wasn't my particular mission to let the world know about anything that was true.

'I'm very interested,' I said. 'Especially if it's anything like Lafcadio Hearn.'

'Good,' said the man, breaking into a grin. I wasn't ready for that. His gum-less teeth were dark and overlapping like stones pushed askew in the ground by tree roots.

'Go ahead and take a seat.'

'Thank you.' He sat down with a small bow of politeness. 'Before I launch in, I'd better ask you if you know what butoh is.'

I shook my head and he allowed himself a quick smile at my ignorance.

'No? Well, butoh is a type of Japanese dance that came from peasant rites in the villages, centuries ago. Its form symbolised the twisting roots beneath the earth. Its other name is the Dance of Darkness.'

I asked him to spell butoh so I could look it up on the Internet later.

'So, the Dance of Darkness. You've got me hooked now,' I said.

I got a harsh look from him. Flippancy wasn't his kind of thing.

'Anyway, about two years ago,' he continued, 'I was living in Prague when a Japanese photographer friend of mine, Eigi, who has since died, arrived in the city. He'd been commissioned to take shots of the Old Town and only planned to stay a few weeks. One day he persuaded me to come with him to a Japanese festival at the Museum of Asian and Oriental Culture. I remember that day feeling bored. Museums are so stuffed with dead things, aren't they?

'But in the evening, we saw the butoh dancer for the first time and, I swear to you, that man danced round those objects and lit them sky-high. I'd never seen anything comparable. His skin was painted white and he was naked but for a white loincloth and his movements were of fire and earth. He looked like a pagan Jesus. I can't express it to you fully, but one woman said to me, "He dances the deepest emotions of the human soul." Eigi took photo after photo of him. Afterwards he introduced himself to the dancer and we all went for a meal together. The dancer's name was Yukio and he was a very quiet, unassuming man. Yet even that night, I saw that Eigi was enraptured by him. Eigi knew from the first moment he saw Yukio that they would collaborate artistically and make one another great.

'Yukio had a few more performances in Prague before moving on to Berlin and Eigi photographed them all. The photographs captured Yukio's shapes so perfectly that European magazines snapped them up. Yukio chose Eigi as official photographer for all his publicity and within months he trusted Eigi's judgement on everything. Where Yukio had previously fused the butoh tradition with some elements of modern dance, Eigi directed him back to a purer form of butoh. I once saw Yukio screaming at his wife who was just trying to help. "I trust only Eigi now," he yelled while Eigi smiled silently from the sidelines. I couldn't help thinking that such an intense relationship was unhealthy for them both.

'Eigi let me in on his vision for Yukio's performance. He dreamed of him dancing in a Christian graveyard lit up by candles. "No one will ever have seen anything more beautiful. I want it all blue, twilight blue."

'"I can't see it happening," I told Eigi point-blank. "Who's going to let you use a graveyard? Haven't you heard of hallowed ground?" He was surprised at my reaction because his experience from Prague was that no one cared for the symbols of Christianity anymore. I began to feel really uneasy about this *succès de scandale* he had in mind.

'A few weeks later, Eigi rang to say he'd found his graveyard. It was in a village outside Prague and had already been hired out once to an American film company. He said to me triumphantly, "I told you religion was dead here. The only thing they worship is the dollar. I told you it's not like Japan."

'He hurled himself into the project, plunging his earnings from photography into it. He wanted it to be a one-off, never to be repeated, and he invited all the influential people in the art world to witness his vision.

'It was September about a year ago when I arrived in the village for the performance. There were posters of Yukio everywhere and I heard a lot of foreign accents. It seemed incongruous with this small village surrounded by hills of wild-headed firs. There was something folkloric about this place with the ringing of the church bell, the giant wooden stakes in the fields and the farmers riding past on long, coffin-shaped carts that carried logs. And for all Eigi's words about the death of religion, there was a crucifix above the bed in the room where I stayed.

'As the day darkened, log smoke thickened the air. I walked up the road, the blue sky glittering above the hills, sloping, solid like ... like the backs of sleeping beasts. The graveyard stood separately from the little church. Two tall spotlights had been set up on either side. They gave a strong light though it was broken in places by the blue-grey of the headstones. White candles were flickering on the graves. Can you imagine? A few hundred people stood within the walls and many of the villagers themselves had come to watch. 'Everyone hushed. The long chords of medieval church music rang out for the first time. We looked towards the gate and Yukio stepped out of the trees onto the path that led into the graveyard. He walked at a slow, measured pace with his head bowed. It made the emotion swirl in your heart. The second his foot touched the grass, he started to dance, throwing himself on the graves like he was longing to join the dead, his fingers bending into the claw shape of tree roots, the veins sprouting under his skin. I swear to you, his muscles breathed like they were alive. He wove and twisted through the gravestones, full of strange seizures, epiphanies of motion. We all watched entranced as he suddenly became aware of us and danced up to people like this ...'

The man, carried away by his own story, leapt up and reached across my desk touching my shoulder lightly, '... and laid his hand on them, before spinning away to the next person. It was as though he wanted everyone there to be touched by his art. Then, as the last chords chimed, he walked out of the graveyard.

'Even after the music stopped, the crowd was silent. Suddenly they exploded. Mad applause! We waited for him to come back to receive his plaudits. I saw Eigi disappear to go and find him but a minute later he came back alone.

'Eigi spoke to everyone, explained that the artist was shy but would be at the restaurant later to accept the acclaim. The crowd filed away, buzzing. I went up to Eigi and said I'd help find Yukio. Eigi was shaking.

'"I know where he is," he said. "Come with me."

'We turned off the white path into the trees. The spotlights from the graveyard gave us enough light and anyway we didn't need it. The white paint on the body shone out between the trees. Yukio was lying there, collapsed. He gave a faint moan.

'"Feel him. He is quite cold," said Eigi and the horror grew in his quiet voice like a wave on a lake. "He's never cold when he dances. It was not Yukio dancing."'

The man fell into silence.

'My God,' I said, waking from the grip of his words. 'So, who or what was the dancer?'

He shrugged. 'When Yukio came to, he remembered nothing of the dance. But that wasn't quite the end because one by one all of those people who'd been tapped on the shoulder that night died. They fell victim to a slow and terrible wasting disease. Eigi himself died this summer.'

He coughed suddenly, elongating the hollows in his cheek. I could see his tongue, almost painfully red behind his pale lips.

A feeling of doom treacled down my back.

'You were one of the ones to be touched, weren't you?'

'The last in line,' he admitted. 'Well,' he said, getting to his feet. 'I hope you will make a good story from it. You know, I don't regret being there that night. To have seen something that no one else will ever see.'

'Wait,' I said, as he walked to the door. I had so many questions. I didn't even know his name.

'Now, that's living,' he said, smiling to himself, and shut the door behind him.

I tried to go after him but he was stepping out of the building, moving with a speed unbelievable for a sick man.

I watched him go. Who really was this man? Was he Yukio or Eigi or …? I recalled his touch on my shoulder and a swathe of revulsion and fear shivered through me.

Drift

Jean O'Brien

Swell on the water under a darkening sky, shivering
in a floundering rubber rib being washed
neither forwards nor back as winds lift, men slick
with sweat tinker with the spluttering engine by a pinprick
of light
from an iPhone and exhausted women shush fractious babies.
Drenched children's eyes widen with fright
as they bail rising water with clay bowls from home.
Holding the vessels of themselves all scan the barely visible
horizon through waves and spray of spindrift for sight of land,
any terra firma will do.

They do know as we know, that land too can be a grave,
a trap, a place to die like any other. We teach it to our children
dry and warm in school, recite Kavanagh's poem –
'The Great Hunger' so they will understand, tell of how we died
in our thousands in the conacre fields and on roadsides.
Our one precious crop failed. We too fled the land,
left the lean roads and dark bog, carried winter with us,
weaselled our way into other places, tasted new air, tested
new earth, almost out of our depths we cast off the old scripts,
survived, landed and eventually thrived.

Straits

Neil Hegarty

Finally, Sarah is henpecked into it. Is how she feels, as she watches her daughter's set lip and righteous eye. Henpecked, unwilling – and yet she has no choice. Ruth has a stake in this story, she says: she has claims, and they are too voluble to ignore.

Her newly commandeered language – of therapy, processing, healing – is undeniably galling. Sarah has never had healing herself. She has simply got on with things, and she has managed well enough, hasn't she? Can't other people do the same? Does Ruth need to know the facts 'in order to have healing'?

Can't she heal herself?

'What?' Sarah had exclaimed, when Ruth used this line for the first time. 'So this is what they're telling you now?'

'Actually,' said Ruth, 'it's what I think too. I need,' she added, 'a map of my world.'

Sarah closed her eyes, opened them, rallied. 'And what about emotional manipulation? What do they say about that?'

Nothing, apparently: Ruth pursed her lips and retreated. But this was a feint, for today she is on the offensive again: and suddenly, her mother feels too exhausted to resist. She looks out at grey London skies, then around the kitchen. She sits.

'I don't want to tell you about this,' she says. 'This advice you're getting, Ruth – it's all wrong.' Some stories are better forgotten; sometimes there is no healing to be had. Or scant healing at best.

Ruth sits too and says something now about individuality: really, she has all the terms right there on the tip of her tongue; no wonder she has ground her mother into submission. Sarah closes her eyes – and now Ruth says something else.

'You owe me,' she says – and the sound of the words, the force of the memory, fall into Sarah's mind.

But where does it begin? Perhaps it began in the early hours: being shaken awake by Mother in September darkness and told to get dressed. 'As quickly as you can,' said Mother, and she turned to wake Hanna, asleep in the next bed. Sarah lay, blinking at the darkness, and Mother glanced around.

'*Now,*' she said and her tone – 'she was not a woman to raise her voice, your grandmother; she never had the need' – roused Sarah instantly. 'No lights,' Mother said, 'and nobody touch the blinds.' Hanna whinged: how could she find her clothes in the dark? 'You'll manage,' Mother said. 'We'll all manage.' She sounded satisfied. *I knew this would happen,* she seemed to say. Remember tonight, her voice carrying across the years: if you ever feel too comfortable in your home, in your surroundings, in your skin, if a future awaits either of you – if it does, then remember tonight.

They were waiting in the narrow hall: Mother and Father and four little bags by the door. One bag each, and no questions – and even Hanna knew now to say nothing as Mother jammed a hat on her head. A gentle knock. 'Hat for you too, Miss,' Father told Sarah, 'we'll be cold before we get there,' and he opened the door.

Mr Sørensen stood on the step. 'He'll be driving us,' murmured Mother to Hanna. Mrs Sørensen lurked behind: she saw Mother, pressed a large hessian bag into her hands, vanished into darkness. The bag, it turned out, was full of food: more than enough for their immediate needs. How many years would pass before they could thank her?

Mr Sørensen drove towards the city without lights. Of course, they must have been spotted a hundred times: there were so many vehicles, all kinds of vehicles, making their stealthy way in from the countryside, across the stubbled fields and towards the coast that night and in the nights that followed. So many individuals playing their part in a vast conspiracy. So Sarah understood, later.

Now, Hanna rustled in the darkness.

'Mother.'

'Hush. What is it, Hanna?'

'What was in Mrs Sørensen's bag?'

'I don't know. Have a feel.'

Mother passed the bag along; and Hanna felt around; then she plunged her nose, horse-like, into the bag and sniffed. 'Pork, Mother!' Smoked pork too, if Sarah's nose was any judge; the smell seemed suddenly to fill the car.

'Hush.' Sarah imagined Mr Sørensen blushing in the darkness – poor man – rummage and rummage. A cold clink of glass against the silver ring Hanna wore, another erupting smell. 'Oh!' she said. 'Apple and onion sauce too!'

The car jolted, the darkness pressed, Hanna went on and on about not being able to eat pork. 'Hush!' Mother said again. 'We might soon be happy to eat anything at all.' But now Hanna was content: she'd found apples in the bag too, and rye bread.

Sarah pauses.

'And then what?' Ruth says.

And then what? Naturally, Sarah remembers the hospital, and waiting there in the course of that long day, and then another midnight run through the city and down to the coast; silent blacked-out streets slipping away, without even a glance back; the fish-smelling and fear-smelling hold of the boat; the searchlights on the water during the crossing of the straits, and the lights, bright and bold, of the coast ahead. Darkness, and dark figures pressed around, the tension thrumming palpably in tight spines and gripping hands. The pain between her legs and the pain in her throat too; the silence of the crowd in the boat; and oh, the thankfulness that it was dark, and that everyone was too preoccupied to pay attention to her.

Ruth begins to relax, to uncoil, to glance out at the London roofs and tiles and brick chimneys.

Or, perhaps it begins at the hospital. With the assembled throng – as many as could be gathered together in haste – being lectured by the matron under the rafters, so that everyone would understand exactly what they must and must not do. The chilly light of the autumn dawn; the gulls screaming and squealing outside. 'I would have screamed and squealed too,' Sarah says, 'if we'd been allowed to make the smallest sound.'

Has Ruth had enough? – her mother watches as the girl tastes the altered atmosphere in the room, tastes pain, presses onward. She says, 'And then what?'

And what then? And what then?

Each of these families had been on the move all night; everyone was exhausted. 'You can picture the scene,' Sarah says. 'There we all were, standing around under the attic roof.' The roof was low; some of the taller adults were bent below the rafters; the whole community pressed around by all their little bags, and everyone tense as they listened to the instructions.

The matron surveyed the crowd. 'You *must* stay in the attic; and you must stay in the middle of the room too' – of course, they couldn't risk having anyone glimpsed, framed in either of the two gable windows. These were curtained, with the ban made manifest by makeshift barricades of bed ends and bits of wooden chairs. A precise, methodical operation; every detail covered.

'Do you understand?' the matron asked – not harshly but with a degree of urgency: *they were all citizens together*, she seemed to say as she stood very erect. The community nodded in unison. 'It really is vital that you abide by these rules.' They understood. 'And a toilet,' and she pointed at the landing, at the stairs just climbed. 'Only one, I'm afraid.'

But beggars could not be choosers. They were being herded, and they knew it – for all that it was being done courageously, valiantly. Sarah knew it: a coldness crept up and down her spine as the matron spoke.

All very clear, then.

And yet, and yet – late in the afternoon, when nobody was looking, she slipped downstairs. (Ruth stares.) The effect of that room under the rafters, stuck with the herd, the old people and the children, the dense, close smell of musty bodies; a change of scene was necessary. 'I needed a break,' she tells Ruth, 'that was all.'

That was all.

Nor does Ruth need every last pitiless detail of what happened next. This Muswell Hill psychologist of hers can say what he likes on this point: he is talking rubbish. Ruth doesn't need to finger every last little jagged shard of knowledge until the blood flows.

Sarah had barely started to make her way along the lower corridor – still in stockinged feet, soundless on the glossy parquet floors – when he appeared at the other end. In white uniform, an orderly, perhaps: she froze. He glanced at the stairs behind her and then at her – and then he smiled, held up an index finger. A command, to remain where she was; and Sarah stood still as he walked towards her, the full length of that polished corridor. He reached her, opened a door, beckoned again.

Ruth stares. 'What did you do?'

Stupid girl. She followed him into the darkness.

Now, she looks at her daughter. 'More?' Ruth says nothing.

Sarah backed into a wall. A shelf pressed against her head. 'Please,' she whispered. 'Let me go upstairs.'

He shook his head. He murmured, 'You owe me.' The shelf pressed terribly into her head.

'And that was where you were conceived.' She went on. 'Your grandparents just upstairs.' Brooms and mops hanging neatly in ranks on the walls. 'Plain wooden shelving. Plain brackets. Are these the details he's been craving, up on Muswell Hill?' But Ruth says nothing.

And at the end, the orderly pointed at the ceiling, put his fingers to his lips – and left, his footsteps squeaking a little on the polished floor. The smell of detergent, the softness of dry mop heads as she moved her fingers through the darkness. The contract signed and sealed: he wouldn't say a word if she wouldn't.

After a moment, she emerged into the long corridor, ran her fingers through her hair, straightened herself, slipped upstairs into the stuffy heat of the attic room. Her father had a book in his hand, her mother was busy with Hanna; nobody had noticed her leave, and nobody remarked on her return.

And that was that: for of course she could never say a word to anyone. How could she?

She has kept her silence – in Sweden, and then in London. For too long, perhaps. Perhaps it does make some sense to go through this exercise. Now she looks around the kitchen and feels a rush of – what? A rousing, heady rage. This is *my* story, she thinks, *my* experience, *my* history; and I never had a say in it. I had to forget what happened to me, for the sake of my tribe.

She clears her throat. 'But maybe I can see where your therapist is coming from.'

She meant to speak gently, but it has come out wrongly – or perhaps correctly, for her voice seems amplified. Here Ruth sits: here is the map of the world that she demanded – and now Sarah feels a sudden rush of pity for her daughter.

She says: 'Do you understand now?' Ruth nods. The two women gaze at each other; Sarah leans forward in her chair.

'This isn't yours. This is *my* story, *my* life,' she says. 'For better or worse, it belongs to *me*.' She pauses again. 'Take what you need from it – but don't you see? You must make your own life,' she says, 'from scratch.'

In September 1943 the government of Nazi-occupied Denmark was tipped off that the German authorities were on the verge of rounding up and deporting to the concentration camps the country's Jewish community. In the days that followed and in conditions of secrecy, the great majority of Danish Jews were spirited across the sea to refuge in Sweden. It is estimated that, out of a total population of approximately eight thousand Danish Jews, some sixty died in the course of World War Two.

Time

Maria McManus

The days
are long gone
since we made
sundials
on the beach

      with
      stones, shells
         a stick
      the obliging sun,
      and here we are

orbiting

still navigating
space
time,
the unknown.

Piddocks

Nuala O'Connor

'Look for pocked stones,' Mariah says, and I obey my sister, for she is never wrong. I follow her across the dark beach, the moon a porthole in the ship of the sky above us. 'You take that way, Cattie, and I shall take this,' she says and, reluctantly, I turn from her and go towards the shore.

I hold my lantern low and scour the sand for wormy rocks; my foot slides on wrack and I right myself hastily. I lift my eyes and watch the beacon that is Mariah drift to the shelter of the cliff. My belly rages and I'm glad I cannot hear its growl for, somehow, listening to the hunger is worse: it champs like a monster at my innards and my mind, both. I wonder if the stomach and the brain are yoked in some way and resolve to ask Mariah. She knows much.

It is a bitter night and my fingers are rigid; my toes are so perished as to be forgotten. I walk, listen to wind and sea-roar, and pray for a morsel to feed on. Ahead I spy a rock with tiny caves all through it. I run, drop to my knees on the sand and set down my lantern. The sea bellows behind me, but I lift the rock and set to my task and peer into each hole until I am rewarded by the bone-glow of a shell. I take my knife, poke it in and prise the shell open but it is empty, the muscly meat long gone. I throw the rock and the shell on the sand and let out a cry of rage. I'm surprised by the sound of my despair – it's like the last rattle of our father before we left him on his bed, as cold as flag, to make for the seashore.

'There we will find food,' Mariah had said, 'as sure as eggs.' She gasped at the sound of that word, eggs; the hunger had been so long with us that an egg was but a half-remembered joy.

We walked far to get here and we saw many dead on the road and some so close to dying that they would be cadavers within hours. Mariah took me under her cloak and ushered me forward, telling me always, 'We'll find something to eat, Cattie, I give you my word.'

I hear a clamour and look to the shoreline, thinking the water means to rise and smother me, but I cannot see it. I strain my eyes back towards the cliffs and find the back-and-forth swing of Mariah's lantern. Its light is tiny and panic claws me: she's so far away. I scramble, grab my own lantern, and make for her. The hem of my gown is wet and, when I look around, I see that the lacy edge of the sea has gained on me, determined to pursue me across the sand. I gallop ahead and it drops back, but once more it blusters up and boils over my feet. I run now as fast as my numb legs will allow.

When I near my sister, I stop; she looks queer and quaint, like a spirit. Her skin is luminescent – there are sparkles all around her mouth and it is as if she has eaten of stars and they dribble now from her lips.

'Mariah?' I say. She holds up her hands and they shimmer too, green and yellow, eerie and beautiful in the night air. 'You look like a phantom.'

'Piddocks, Cattie!' she says, 'I found fresh piddocks. They are just as Father described.' Her fingers are candles that she holds out to me, her face is a beatific orb. I clamber to her side and she begins to feed me, placing the tiny clams between my lips. 'Chew with care,' she says, 'take your time.'

The piddocks hit my tongue in a salty rush, they find my belly and expand it. 'More, I need more,' I cry.

Mariah puts another clam on my tongue and one on her own. 'We are safe now, Cattie,' she says.

I look up at her. My sister is the angel of the sea, the bright balefire to which I always go for shelter, for succour, for warmth. We stand under the cliff together, consuming each piddock with rapt attention, feeling our stomachs glow. Behind us, while we eat our fill, the black sea closes in.

Portrait of a Real Woman

Geraldine O'Kane

As I make my way into the water, a woman in her sixties is being helped up the steps on the other side, two men holding her arms and the male instructor pushing her from behind. I wonder what keeps bringing her back. It's only later as we are doing squats by the edge of the pool, I find myself faced with the cubicle she still occupies. We are only permitted in the shallow end and although I try to avert my eyes, from the two-foot gap along the bottom of the poolside changing booth, I watch her repeatedly try to hoist her socks and eventually her underwear onto her own frame with her walking stick. It is almost thirty minutes after her session ends when she opens the door and makes her way out of the pool area.

Penrose never-
ending-staircase,
we are illusion's edge.

Slip

Mia Gallagher

Baltic, I thought. Something about her cheekbones and the eyes, and the long slight build, and her skin. Though mostly, it was the hair. Once you're into November and the mercury's below nine and you've hair of any length, you're mad to go in without a cap. Even if you did, you'd never duck your head under or keep it there. Not for a good length of time, not unless you were used to real cold.

That morning the water was gnawing chunks off the pier, retching it back at the land. Blocks of aggregate scattered on the jetty, black weed wound around them. Stinking brown algae sliming the surface of the slips. Nobody was in. I'd cycled and the sweat was already cooling on my back. The surf pounding and the only safe place to go in was between the small steps and the Rock. Then I saw the wee dark head. Like a dog, the little one in that painting Tom used to talk about, a head, over an invisible body, struggling through a mass of yellow. She was just bobbing there, waiting. A wave would come but instead of leaping, she'd duck her head, dive into its heart, let it crash through her.

We're a chatty lot here. Plenty to say about nothing. Ciarán's the worst, bores us silly with his yammer. If you try to bring it round to yourself, he'll just wash over you, oblivious. Unless you're a man, he'll listen to a man. But we all talk. It's the fear, and the cold, that building apprehension during the change. We always test each other: So how is it today? Someone says a number, and then there's the comparison. Oh. Worse than yesterday, better than Sunday, cooler today only it didn't feel it with the sun. The girl with the little dog's head never chatted. I tried smiling once, the second time I saw her. She smiled back, but it was a don't-come-further sort of smile. You get to know what smiles mean out here.

There was a real push to it when I got in, and a suck too. Not a rip, but nearly. It kept tugging me down to the Rock though I wasn't doing much, so it didn't tug far. I just jumped, like I was a kid, ten in Tramore with my granny. My feet numb from the frost on the sand, and I'd left my flip-flops at the top of the steps, under one of the bits of pier the water had coughed up. I'd thought I'd stay in a while, not long enough to be stupid, but enough to sort out my head. I assumed she'd come out before me, because she'd been in when I arrived. But as I climbed out, taking care on the steps because it was at that tricky point, wave in meeting wave out, crests amplifying, I saw she was still there. Head wet, hair dripping; waiting, ducking.

Another ten minutes, then she got out, a slip of a thing in football shorts and a sports bra.

*

The next time, Ciarán was there. It was wild again, even more, too wild to go in by our usual slip near the Tower, so we headed down to the steps. Ciarán went in at the fourth ones, nearest the Rock, and I went in at the small ones, because that was where Tom used to go, Tom who couldn't swim out of his depth.

I went out further that day, lifting my feet from the sand. The girl with the little dog's head was there again. She'd been near the steps when we got in, but now she was closer to the Rock. Maybe the water had moved her, maybe she'd moved herself. She wasn't even inside a Gorgeous-isn't-it? shouting distance.

Ciarán was bobbing, anxious. He gets anxious, like small men sometimes do, when his manhood looks like it might be in question. Ah I didn't do much, I knew he'd tell me afterwards, before offering me a biscuit which I wouldn't take, because biscuits were Tom's job to remember. Ah I only did a bit, he'd say, there's no point doing too much, right? but without waiting for an answer, because he doesn't listen to women, and if I wasn't careful and he wasn't either, he might then say How's himself? and at that there'd have to be a laugh and a Jesus I'll forget my own name next. Ha very ha, I'd want to say then, but he probably wouldn't get it.

*

The third time, it was like glass. Bitter, and though there wasn't a wind, the air had edge. The tide was in, almost to the top of the Rock. She went in a few minutes after me, down our slip. No hat again, and from the feel it was seven, and at the start of the winter that's cold, though by February it's grand. She did a few strokes of crawl, then breaststroke, and she reminded me even more of a dog, jerking forward the way breaststroke does when it's not done properly, little head craning, wet hair stringy down her neck. The time before, she'd been in a bikini – olive green with a flower pattern, nice – but this time she was back in the shorts and the sports bra. The water so cold it burnt my hands. I hadn't brought my gloves or booties though I knew I wouldn't be able to hold off much longer.

I'd gone out towards the buoy, which I wouldn't reach again till summer, doing the crawl mainly, face-out, only dipping the eyes in once or twice. Then I headed back via the first steps, in a triangle. She'd gone in after me that time, so when I came out I didn't feel bad to see she was still there. I had to change fast as my body was lobster, patches of orange over my knees, and the trick is to fool the core – let it ride on its rush, imagine itself hot, then pull the gear on fast before what's inside realises all its heat has scooted out, to warm the fingers and the toes.

I was busy, wanting to get the gear on before my fingers stopped working, but not so busy I didn't allow myself a small moment of satisfaction to see that the girl with the dog's head was heading towards the second steps, the easy ones, only a short arc from the slip

because the time before, when it had that even stronger suck, so strong you could hardly crawl back against it, she'd struggled around to those same steps, the second ones, and got out there and I'd thought, with a certain smugness, Ha, and kept on for the first steps, which were further, but the water was coming in too fast too hard, bashing me away from them around towards the nook

and then I couldn't help remembering last winter, after Tom went off to that place, and I'd gone in when it was wild and the annoying Czech fella had told me to go down the first steps

because it was madness on the slip, utter madness

and the Czech said, Go down the shore side of the rail, Karen, not the water side, and stupidly, I'd listened, and once I was in, it had taken me, churned me, flinging me towards the nook, the dangerous corner where steps meet pier, and telling myself don't panic, I'd reached with my feet and found a ledge, and climbed up, gripping the bockety concrete, disregarding the offer of a helping hand from the annoying Czech, Mr Gallant yeah right

and this had gone through my head the second time I saw the girl, the time with the bikini and the even stronger suck, me reaching for the rail at the bottom of the first steps and getting batted back, batted back, shoved instead towards the nook and the razor hidden rocks, and in the end I had to force myself to swallow my smugness and give up, and follow the invisible strokeprints of the girl with the little dog's head and scramble like a toddler up the second steps

so this last day, when it was like glass, I'd expected her to do the easy thing and get out there again, at the second steps, making her total stay in the water, both time and distance, shorter than mine. While I was changing, she'd left my field of vision, disappearing behind the shelter wall, and it was only when I went to the bars to twist out my togs that I saw her, but not climbing out or loping along the concrete, no, she was still in, beyond the second steps, heading to the third ones, the small ones. Tom's steps. A face-down crawl, then she'd stop, duck, shake her head, and bob for a bit, hair wringing in seven degrees. I didn't time her but it was very long to be that cold. When I finished the togs, I dialled Tom's number. It went straight to voicemail, like I knew it would. I hung up before the beep. By then, she was on her way back. Her face and head crimson-sore and her eyes in the water, not every stroke, just one or two at a time, but that was plenty.

I passed her on my way out of the shelter. She was struggling a bit with the gear. Her face had gone greyish and she didn't look what I'd call warm.

*

It took a while to load the bike. By the time I was done, the girl had changed and was walking away. Dressed, she had lovely legs, very long and delicate. She was wearing boots to just above the knee with a little lip that turned over. She was probably in layers bundled up though I couldn't see what was under the coat. It seemed like a good coat. All in black, except for earmuffs, or maybe they were headphones, grey and fluffy, and a scarf. She hoisted her bag onto her shoulder and went down past the nice houses towards the railway bridge.

I had to go the other way because of the bike. I stood full weight hammering down on the pedals to beat the hill and I was thirteen again. On the main road I cheated and took the footpath. I was cycling fast. A figure came out of the opening at the railway bridge and I pedalled harder. I couldn't bear to believe she'd walked the distance quicker than I'd cycled it. My head was still stupid from the water and when I got close, I realised the gait was different. There were no boots with lips and the jeans were green. Nor was it such a tall person and there was no lope. No wet head hitting the six-but-feels-like-three November air.

I passed it, the walker, whoever it was.

At the station I decided to bring the bike down the stairs, though there was no rush because the train wouldn't be there for another seven minutes and I could have used the lift. I was awkward and caught the bike in the wrong place and my balance wavered.

Do you want a hand? said a voice behind me. A young woman's.

No, I said, too fast too hard. I hoisted the bike and got it right.

At the bottom of the stairs I turned, wanting to be nice again. It wasn't her but another girl in black, less of a slip and wearing shoes with no socks.

Thank you, I said, and made a joke to show I knew how to hoist a bike, even at my age. Glad after all it wasn't her, so the joke and the Thank you were real. Then I dialled Tom's number again as the train approached, and let the empty digital space after the beep fill with the squealing brakes, remember me, sweetheart, remember me, and I thought of the girl with the little drowning dog's head jerking through quicksand, and her face was a sunset, burning.

Degrees of Separation

Maurice Devitt

Today it's your turn to walk
your son to school, stand
on the step in the mizzling dark,
like a paperboy waiting to be paid,
while she prepares his lunch,
straightens the collar of his coat
and issues her final, clipped instructions,
before opening the door and passing him
wordlessly into your world, secure
in the knowledge that she has packed
his favourite sandwiches
and that ten minutes talking about the match
will never be enough
to deflect from last night's tears.

Reuben

John O'Donnell

Mam says if she finds whoever did this to me, she'll swing for him.

You mean them, I think. *The Twins.* Though I don't say this.

I glance around the day room of the Rehab. Two of the other lads in wheelchairs are at a table, playing cards.

'That fool Sergeant Nyhan, has he done anything? Would you not speak to him, Sean?' Mam says, her eyes welling as she turns towards my da.

When she starts up with this talk, though, Da looks out the window and says nothing. I thought at first it might be the shock of seeing me like this, but now I'm not so sure. Maybe someone's said something. Maybe he knows.

Actually, Nyhan did come in one time to see me.

'Well, Donie,' he said, sitting down beside the bed I was lying in, 'is there anything you want to say to me?'

'Sure, I already told ye,' I said. 'I can remember nothing before ye found me at the bottom of the quarry.'

He eyed up the wheelchair in the corner and then looked back at me.

'Would you like to make a statement, Donal?' he said, taking out his notebook; real formal, real sincere. 'We can do nothing without a statement.'

I think part of him really wants to get the ones responsible. But something else behind those hooded eyes was saying as he looked at me, *Well, Donie, I'm sorry for you, boy, but by Jesus you deserved it.*

I don't think Fonsie Meaney liked me anyway. It wasn't just my working down in Burger King at the Plaza; no man was ever going to be good enough for his Aoife. His only daughter – only child, in fact – and with Aoife's mam long gone, there was just the two of them for years. Like husband and wife, they were. Fonsie knew me from around, though I wasn't a punter so I never went into his shop. Meaneys. As a name for a bookies, it was pure class. Pure gold, too; when he sold the shop to Boylesports, the word in Queally's was he was minted. He'd enough anyway to build the house up on the hill for us, and to put a white tent in his garden for the big day. 'You take care of her now,' he said during his speech, the big silk-waistcoated gut of him turning towards me, 'do you hear me, Donie?'

'I will, surely,' I said.

Aoife sniffled then and squeezed my hand.

But there was no blub out of Fonsie. He just looked at me, head cocked, like he was aiming down the barrel of a gun.

If there was one thing Fonsie and I agreed on, though, it was that neither of us was gone on the baby's name. I'm sure Fonsie had been hoping for Alphonsus, and my own da would've loved if we'd called him Sean. I don't even know how Aoife came up with it; she just announced it one night when we were sitting up in the big new house waiting for her to pop.

'What about Reuben?' she said.

'Where'd you get *that*?' I said.

'Don't know,' she said, her hand smoothing her bump. 'But I like it.'

He always slept really well. I'm no expert, but after three months he was sleeping through five hours a night, which everyone reckoned was pretty good. That wasn't the problem; the problem was when he was awake. We took him to the clinical psychologist when he was two. We went private. Fonsie paid. The psychologist had a pair of glasses on a chain around her neck. She told us to keep a diary of every time Reuben screamed or rocked himself in the corner or refused to make eye contact. She also asked us about our family medical histories, especially the mental stuff, because there's often what she called 'a genetic component'. 'Triad' was another word she used, 'triad of impairments'. And 'spectrum'. When she told us a year later that Reuben was 'on the spectrum', Aoife began to weep. 'What do you mean, *spectrum?*' she said. I put my arm around her, but she was somewhere else completely. I'd say she already knew: she'd looked it up on Google, even though the psychologist had advised us not to. Reuben was sitting on the floor beside the desk, playing with a paper-puncher and some sheets of paper. He didn't even look up when Aoife started crying.

The psychologist was saying this was difficult news and a very difficult time for everyone. She talked about getting more multidisciplinary assessments, and an SNA when he started school, but all I could hear was the little click each time Reuben punched out another hole, until the floor was covered with hundreds of small white discs and there were no sheets of paper left.

Fonsie wanted to sue: the hospital, the nurse who gave the vaccine, the vaccine company, the works. But the psychologist told him not to bother. My da just looked confused when we told him. He'd have grown up with lads who were strange or touched or had a bit of a want on them: no one mentioned 'autism' then, because there was no such thing. Mam seemed to know a bit about it, though. 'Well,' she said quietly to Da one evening when I'd called over, 'if it's the genes, it's not from our side.' As I strapped Reuben into his car seat outside their house, the little voice I'd heard before in my head started whispering a bit louder: *Supposing he's not yours?* Because there was that fella Kearney that Aoife'd always been sweet on, even in school. He was never out of Boylesports, apparently, filling out betting slips and mooning over Aoife, who still worked there. And Aoife was always better at calming Reuben when he got upset. When I tried, he'd just turn away, with no let-up in the screeching.

See, there'd be lads around the town who'd say I was a bit of a hard man. *The bould Donie.*

Well, maybe.

I wouldn't go looking for trouble, and it wouldn't come looking for me.

But the one thing those bar-stool experts down in Queally's would agree on is that the last thing I'd ever do is to hit a woman.

Or a child.

So I need to explain.

I'd just finished a double shift, see, and I really needed a kip, but as I put my key in the front door, I knew there was no way I'd be able to sleep with that racket.

'Can you make him stop,' I said, heading for the stairs.

'Are you not coming in to say hello?' said Aoife from the kitchen. 'To your *son*.'

So I looked in, like she asked. The floor was covered with pots and pans and saucers and plates, and he was sitting there, banging away with a pair of wooden spoons. Already a couple of the plates were broken.

'Stop it, please, for the love of Jesus,' I said, and I hunkered down in front of him.

'Sure, what harm?' said Aoife. She was at the counter mixing beans and weeds some website had recommended in his bowl.

I tried to look him in the eye, but he turned away and started hammering even harder.

'Reuben, please,' I said.

God, he did look a bit like Kearney.

'*You* stop, Donie,' said Aoife, laughing, 'you're the one who's shouting.'

I grabbed him by the shoulders, and I shook him. Once. Twice, maybe. I wasn't trying to hurt him; I was just trying to get him to let go of those spoons and give us all a moment's peace. But he started screaming and trying to twist out of my grip, and that's how he hit his head off the leg of the table.

'You leave him alone!' said Aoife, and she flew at me. She was pulling at me to make me let him go, and as I yanked my arm away, I hit her – pure accident – with my elbow. She slumped onto the floor, and as she lay there among all the pots and pans, the corner of her left eyebrow was already starting to swell.

I didn't mean to. Of course I didn't. Nothing like this ever happened before, and it would never happen again – that's what I kept telling her as she sat up and started checking Reuben for bruises. There wasn't a mark on him.

'He just got a fright,' I said, and I tried to hug the pair of them, but she just pushed me away.

I got a bag of frozen veg and held it to her eyebrow.

'Peas,' said Reuben, pointing at the bag. 'Peas peas peas peas peas.'

Then he started off with the wooden spoons again.

'You go lie down,' I said. 'I'll look after him.'

'No way,' said Aoife, taking the bag of peas off me. 'I'm not leaving him here.'

I stood up. Maybe I was better going upstairs and leaving the pair of them at it until things got back to normal.

'I love you,' I said. 'You know that, don't you?'

But she wouldn't look at me.

'Yeah,' she said.

The next day, as the bruise above her eye began to bloom, she put some make-up on it. 'We can say you fell,' I said, though she was never much of a one for keeping secrets. Maybe it was Kearney she told, though with all he's spending on the ponies down in Boylesports, he wouldn't have had the spondulicks to pay the Twins. Or maybe she told Fonsie. Daddy's little girl, and all that. Anyway, three nights later I was walking up the hill from Queally's after closing when a car went by me, and then stopped.

The driver got out first. The taller one. I don't know who christened them 'the Twins'; they aren't even brothers. 'Howiya, Donie,' he said.

The smaller stockier one got out then and stood in front of me. They were both wearing the black security uniforms they wore at the Plaza.

'Howiya, lads,' I said.

The back passenger door was ajar, and I could see something in the footwell; a wheel brace.

'Would we go for a bit of a spin?' the taller one said.

He was behind me now, a brick shithouse; no way would I've got past him.

'Lads,' I said, 'I think there's been some class of a mistake.'

Beyond the ditch there were just fields. Even if I'd let out a roar, there wasn't a sinner who'd have heard me.

'Get in, Donie,' said the taller one.

The smaller one sat beside me in the back. The taller one jumped in behind the wheel, pressed the central locking and started the engine.

Then the car climbed slowly up the hill and turned right, heading for the quarry.

Mam says the main thing is for me to get better. The bungalow herself and Da live in is small, but with a bit of work it could be made wheelchair-friendly when the time comes. She never mentions Aoife.

And I do ask about Reuben. It means 'Behold, a son'. I looked it up.

The last time I asked about him, though, Mam just shook her head. 'Poor Reuben,' she said sadly. 'That poor, poor boy.'

'Do you think maybe you could bring him in to see me?' I said. Because, actually, I missed him.

'Well now, Donie,' said Mam, sitting up real straight, 'I'm not sure if that'd be *appropriate*.'

Straight away she knew she'd hurt me. She put her hand on my arm and started stroking it. 'Sure, he wouldn't be able for all the carry-on in here,' she said, trying to make it up with me.

Da was still doing his peering-out-the-window thing. I saw them glancing at each other, though, and I knew then that she knew now as well. But she kept stroking my arm anyway, and I just kept looking down at the day-room carpet tiles.

Fifty Years Later

Brian Kirk

'Perhaps my best years are gone. When there was a chance of happiness. But I wouldn't want them back. Not with the fire in me now.'

–Samuel Beckett, *Krapp's Last Tape*

A new wind shakes
the green branches
as you shuffle along.
How the weeks have flown
since Easter, blown like
April blossoms, like petals
from the early rose, dull fires
on dewy grass
you'll never mow again.
What took you back
to this place after all
these years? Not faith,
or fear of death, or loneliness.
Get up off your knees,
fill up your lungs
and sing the song
you sang so long ago;
confirm spring's resolution
in this summer of your winter.

Profess to fathom wrong
from right, to practise
strength, wisdom and love,
to dream, to strive to be
all things: the lion, lamb
and dove.

I Left That City Years Ago

Niamh Boyce

The storm has driven all sorts in here today; pensioners, mothers and toddlers, workmen in high-vis, stray cats like me. I grab a table next to the door, the last one free. Outside the awnings buckle, release a tide of rain that gushes onto the path before splashing up again. I open the menu intent on finding something filling but slimming when the waiter looms; a guy in a pristine butcher's apron, handsome and polite but so obviously under pressure I order the first thing I see, The Special – an organic goat's cheese tartlet. Before I can change my mind, the waiter has zoomed off again.

A woman touches my shoulder. Hair scraped back, kind expression. Am I waiting for someone? Do I mind if she shares my table? I tell her I'm not, and that I don't. She pulls out a seat for the lady she's with, an elderly woman wearing a tangerine beret. My tartlet arrives. I crush the crust and the aroma that wafts up reminds me of the socks overflowing from the laundry basket at home.

The older woman removes her beret, unpeels a fur-trimmed coat. She has gems on every finger. Vintage jewellery; marcasite and rubies. Such frail glamour next to my denim and parka get-up. But who has time to arrange themselves before stepping out? Lucy, will you stop, lots of people do; you just couldn't be bothered. Snoozing on this morning while the wind crept through the house like a child imitating a ghost. When there were so many things you should've been attending to, those socks for a start.

The two women haven't stopped yapping since they sat down. Ruby Rings waves a chocolate éclair and says something I can't quite catch. Her fingertips are spattered with turquoise paint. Kohl-rimmed eyes crinkle shut when she smiles. The menu slips towards the floor. I bend to pick it up and notice she's wearing Doc Martins. They both are. I suppose we all end up in comfortable footwear. *From Jimmy Choos to flat shoes*, I say to myself. Which is ridiculous. As if I ever wore Jimmy Choos. Me, who's wearing runners (Nike, my sister's) these past few months because of my, oh god, bunion. It brings me great shame. I should go to confession. Bless me Versace for I've sinned, against myself and all others with taste and good eyesight. I've been wearing white runners with slack-arsed denims. Save my soul, I've fallen by the wayside. I'm thinking all this when who swaggers in, drenched and long-haired in her Levi 501s, but my younger self. She strides past my table, then halts and reverses. Squints, moves closer …

'I don't believe it. I just don't believe it. It's not true. You're not me, look at you. Frumpy. Why are you wearing glasses, have you lost your lenses? And where's your eyeliner, have you an infection? And your hair, what have you done to your hair! I thought we agreed we'd wear it past our knees till we're ninety?'

I wish she'd keep her voice down, but the women don't seem to notice. They're bent over a napkin one of them has drawn something on, turning it this way and that.

'Hello? The hair?'

I touch my bare neck. 'Ah, it got in the way. It's easier having it bobbed, with the kids …'

'Kids, what kids? We weren't having any more babies? Only selfish people have children on purpose. Egotists. Have you gone and had more kids on us?'

'Just the two …'

'Oh my god, no wonder you've no waist, have you stopped the yoga with Nina? You really must get back to it.'

She yanks out the seat across from me and sits down, peers at my face as if it's a map. An old one. *Here be monsters,* I think.

'So – have you discovered anything?'

'Like what?'

'The meaning of life, that's what! You know, any pearls of wisdom? No offence, but you must be well on. And no offence again, but I thought I'd be a bit more alluring in my middle years. Well, any wisdom? You must be what, thirty-eight?'

'Forty.'

'No shit. You must've done loads of things by now. Did you buy a cottage by the sea? Have you lived in Paris?' She starts to sing – something about Paris, and a sports car.

She had a terrible voice, bless her.

'Please tell me you've woken up in Paris! Please tell me you've drifted to sleep to the howls of the Atlantic Ocean as turf burnt low in the fire place!'

Terrible voice. But ten out of ten for drama.

'No. Neither. Not yet.'

'Ah, Lucy, what've you been doing all this time?'

'Well, you know with children and everything …'

'How's my little baby doing?'

'Amy's nineteen now, and in college.'

Her eyes well up. She takes out a cigarette.

'Ah, don't cry. She's grand. A great girl. You can't smoke here. It's against the rules.'

She wipes the tears from her face, puts the cigarette behind her ear. I'm not going to tell her what's ahead. The year Amy turned sixteen and ran away. The stress. The fear. I'll leave that out. I don't think she'll be able for it. She worries enough already.

'She's in college? But I'm still trying to get her to sleep through the night.'

She flicks her damp hair. Doesn't even think about grey, or imagine that she'll ever change.

'Any advice about the sleeping, do I find anything that works? Everyone says I should just let her cry, but I can't bear not to pick her up.'

'No. There's no secret. The sleep will happen one night and you'll barely notice; something else will have already taken its place, some other issue.'

I won't tell her about the tantrums, or the loneliness.

'Just … just don't worry so much,' I add, offering the only pearl of wisdom I can.

'Oh. That's great. That's a fucking deadly insight. Any action on the man front or are you living in a lesbian colony with them late-life babies?'

'Not that late.'

She doesn't ask about the younger kids, their names, their ages. Doesn't she care?

'Late enough. Well, any action?'

'I'm with Dave.'

'Who the flying fuck is he?'

'You'll find out, it's a long story.'

'Tell me about him. Is he gorgeous, is he hung like a donkey, does he go like a sewing machine?' She laughs. She laughs like a witch. That much hasn't changed, or so I'm told.

'Stop. I don't talk like that anymore.'

'Ooh, don't you? How long are you two together?'

'Around twelve years.'

'Ah Jesus, Lucy! Twelve years? You're not …' She goes even paler, if that's possible.

'No, don't worry. We're not married.'

'Praise be! Down with the patriarchal institutions, eh girlfriend?'

I don't feel the same enthusiasm but I don't say anything. I don't say, You won't always feel that way. She hears that a lot.

'How old is this guy?'

'Forty-five.'

'An auld lad! It gets worse. Please tell me that you're still painting?'

'Nothing new, not for a while.'

'Did you at least finish the Melusian mermaid?'

I had forgotten about that painting. The figure was missing something – I never knew what. Or maybe it wasn't missing anything, maybe it was overworked. I whited it out in the end, can barely recall how it looked.

'I'll get back to her. Don't worry; she's safe and sound …'

'You'd bloody well better get back to her. Those oils were professional quality; they cost a week's rent. By the way, are you still there?'

'I left the city years ago.'

'Ah, no.'

'Ah, yes. I live in Rath.'

'Please tell me you're lying. I'll throw myself off a cliff before I'll let us live there. What are you doing, living with an auld man in bloody blink-and-you'll-miss-it? What happened? What happened to us?'

There are calls from the street outside. Her name, my name, over and over again. I see them then, a raggle-taggle search party – guys in loose jumpers, with wet curls about their necks – waving in through the window.

She blows them theatrical kisses and rises to her feet. Suddenly, she's hugging me. I inhale her perfume. Vanilla spiked with mandarin and something else, something heady. I resist the urge to tell her to stock up – it can't be got nowadays for money or love. She lets go, pats my arm as if I were the younger one.

'The mermaid. Right?'

'Right.'

With that, she's at the door. Wind stirs through the restaurant as she leaves, tablecloths lift their skirts, napkins flitter to the floor. Then the door shuts, sealing us all in again.

The women at my table have finished without my noticing. They're already moving towards the exit. I notice the napkin then, the one they were drawing on. It lies face down on the table. Biro seeps from the other side in wavy lines. I'm tempted to turn it over but they haven't left yet. The older woman is adjusting her beret by the doorway. She smiles at me. I lift my hand in a small wave and am surprised, though I shouldn't be, when instead of waving back, she winks and blows me a kiss. I place my hand on the napkin as the door slams in her wake. A large soft square of white tissue with blue bleeding through. I press down. My fingers spread wide. I don't need to turn it over, to know who's on the other side.

Cataract Gorge

Stephanie Conn

I've taken both routes to the bridge;
gripped this red suspended metal twice.

Summer. A tan deepening at my neck.
I watched the spot where three rivers meet.
I'd walked the dust track in sandals, turned
my back against rock and pressed my stomach
flat when the trail narrowed to a rope –

I heard the click-clack racket of a hundred beetles
hanging from the tips of trees, disguised as death
black pussy willow. Laughter bubbled in the throats
of children on swings. Leggy teens dived off
a basalt ledge to break the surface of the South Esk.

Spring. These cultivated Victorian gardens
should bloom colour and spray parachute seeds
into the warming air, but everything's cold, sodden.
Paths are slipping out of place. Ferns fluoresce,
as if they've sucked up the sun's radiating flare.

Heavy drops of caught rain clutch each leafy frond.
The swings have been swallowed by the swell –
a muddy torrent, frothing and foaming at the mouth.

The peacocks take cover under the café canopy,
their eyed feathers laid low beside a Coca-Cola sign.

If I'm here again, I'll glide above the basin in a silver
chair-lift, step off by the Japanese maple, the English oak.

Horse Latitudes

Danielle McLaughlin

They park beside the boarded-up lifeguard hut. There's a blanket in the boot and she drapes it over her arm, carries the bag with the sandwiches and water in her other hand. He doesn't offer to carry anything and doesn't remark on the surroundings as much as she'd hoped. But when they reach the sandy path through the dunes, and the long stretch of sea comes into view, he stops and puts his hands on his hips. 'Holy shit,' he says.

'Yes,' she says, gratified. The waves rear up miles out at sea and thunder in with such force that it seems as if they might keep going, over the dunes, up the path to the car park. Seagrass sprouts in hues of green and purple by their feet and there are touches of rust in the reeds.

'I remember a cave that my sister and I used to play in as children,' she says. 'Our parents would bring us here in the summertime and we'd jump out of the car and race to it first thing. We could go there now, if you like?' She glances at him, and notices that he is gazing out to sea. Has he even been listening?

'It's a short walk, if I remember correctly,' she says. 'It would be a nice place to sit and eat.'

He nods. 'Sure. Why not?'

They walk west, the setting sun streaking the sky pink, seagulls whirling and crying overhead. They take off their shoes and socks to wade across a narrow channel to a cluster of rocks. It isn't particularly warm, and she's glad she brought a coat. The shoes and socks are difficult to carry, and the blanket twice slips off her arm.

'Will we be at this place soon?' he says.

'Not far now,' she says, because she can see a jut of cliff face that looks familiar, and the cave, she thinks, is just beyond that. She remembers shimmying with her sister up the cliff face and into the cave. There they'd sit, invisible to anyone on the strand, watching water trickle down the walls while out ahead of them was the bright dazzle of sun on sea.

The approach to the cliff is trickier than she remembers. He doesn't complain, but he doesn't pass comment of any other kind either. It's like marshalling a placid but uninterested child. Finally, the rocks and pools are behind them and they're in a cove of white sand indented with pebbles and shells.

'Here we are,' she says, pleased that they've arrived, that she hasn't led them on a wild goose chase. She turns to the cliff face bearded with wisps of green foliage, tiny blue flowers sprouting in the crevices, and sees that the cave she remembers is not a cave at all. It's better described as a ledge that becomes a narrow tunnel running back into the cliff. It has depth, certainly, but the roof is low, no more than four feet at its highest part, and the width wouldn't fit two adults. It seems impossible to her now that two small girls could have played in there at the same time.

He starts to laugh and, relieved, she laughs too: it's preposterous, the more she thinks about it. Of all the places she could have chosen, she has brought him to this ledge, thick, she sees now, with bird shit and feathers and something grey and crumpled further in that might be a dead seagull. 'Funny,' she says. 'I remember it as being completely different.' She lays out the blanket on the sand and they sit down. *This could be something out of a film*, she thinks, except that she would be played by someone younger and prettier.

She hands him a sandwich and for a while they eat in silence, looking out at the waves. After a few minutes, without saying anything, he puts down his half-eaten sandwich and stands up.

Terrified that he will want to leave, she flails about mentally for something to hold him. Her eyes dart about the shore, the glistening strings of seaweed, the blush of clouds overhead. 'Your house is on fire,' she says, in desperation. 'Your house is on fire and you're allowed back inside to rescue one thing. What would it be?'

He glances down at her, frowns. 'I wouldn't go inside if it was on fire,' he says. 'Obviously.'

'It's hypothetical,' she says. 'Humour me.'

He sighs, but sits back down. 'All right,' he says. 'Let me see.'

Relieved, she takes a tissue from her pocket, busies herself with cleaning sand and mayonnaise from her fingers. Her gaze flickers to the cliff face. How could she ever have thought of that grimy ledge as a cave? How small she must have been, to have ever considered that space big, and how had her parents let them wander alone at that age, what were they thinking? And then she realises that she'd always been completely safe on this beach at the age of six or seven; it is now that she's an adult that she can't be left to her own devices.

'I think I'd rescue my great-great-grand-uncle's letters,' he says, staring out at the ocean. 'The ones he wrote on board ship when he was calm-bound in the horse latitudes.' *She pictures his great-great-grand uncle who looks exactly like him, but in sailor costume from a black-and-white film.*

'Calm-bound?' she says. 'I thought calm was supposed to be a good thing? At sea, I mean.'

'Not on a freight ship with no wind to fill the sails.'

To an onlooker they must seem like any ordinary and happy couple, talking about ordinary things. If they had ham sandwiches instead of brie and salami focaccia, they could be her mother and father. 'It's a pretty name, all the same,' she says. 'Horse latitudes. Is it to do with the horse constellation?'

'You're thinking of the bear,' he says. 'No, it's where they threw horses overboard in the subtropics. To lighten the load. To get moving again.'

At a thirty-degree angle to the equator, his uncle emerges from below deck into a subtropical night fog. He takes a flask from the pocket of his britches, swallows and shivers.

'Wasn't there something else they could have thrown overboard first?'

'What? Like the cabin boys?'

'Like the furniture.'

'Oh yes. Of course. The chaise longues, the bookcases. How much furniture do you think was on board a nineteenth-century cargo ship?'

She opens her mouth to say something, closes it again. She traces a spiral in the sand with her finger, round and round.

The fog of night gives way to haze of day. Outlines of horses emerge, horses of every size, shape and colour, bound for the West Indies. His uncle goes over to a palomino pony, places a hand on its rump.

He sighs, runs a hand through his hair. 'They would only have had so much drinking water. It would have run out if they were calm-bound for too long.'

His uncle puts his mouth to the palomino's ear. 'There isn't enough water,' he whispers. There is a splash, a violent white-foamed thrashing, and then the pony is under. Bubbles from its nostrils rise to the surface. After a while, the bubbles stop.

She stands up, slapping at her thighs to knock the sand from her jeans. 'If *my* house was on fire,' she says, 'I would rescue the pebble from Inch beach that you gave me on our first date.' She wonders if this might even be true, though she knows it's more likely that it's this beach that has caused her to think of the pebble.

He turns to her, seems to register her change in mood. 'Actually,' he says, 'it's possible that the term "horse latitudes" derives from the ceremonial parading of the effigy of a horse, and that no animals were harmed during the making of my family history.'

But she is no longer listening. She's walking away, taking a shortcut through the dunes, not bothering to check if he's following. The waves on the way back are just as majestic, but now their grandeur makes her feel insignificant. They keep roaring in, and she feels that were she to run to them in surrender they wouldn't accept her, they would spit her out onto the sand, roll her back and forth over the shrapnel of shells and glass-edged stones. She shivers and pulls the sleeves of her coat down over her wrists, her balled fists. She switches on the radio as soon as she gets into the car and sits there, watching the speck of his approaching form grow bigger and bigger. He has the blanket slung over his left shoulder, the end trailing in rock pools. She wonders what his great-great-grand-uncle wrote in that letter, and if he ever mentioned horses at all, or if he wrote only about the weather, and the rations, and pretended that everything was fine.

Beaming

Katie Donovan

It's twenty years
since I first watched him –
dextrous and handsome
in his tux – play cello
along with plangent brass;
oboe; the drum roll
of percussion;
innocent of what was to come.
Now I sit with our children,
in the audience again.
My boy: tall, fourteen,
turns to share a smile.
My girl, with her sea-green gaze
and petal cheeks, swims deep
in the swell of sound
and the dance of coloured light.
No high classical here:
we are tuned
to the signature notes
of Spock, Yoda and McFly;
the transports of Hollywood sci-fi.
The players sport costumes,
festive as Solo, Vader, Rey.
In the shelter of the music,

I grieve,
for what was quenched
in the onslaught of disease,
marching
like the stormtroopers of doom.
When the last crescendo dims,
and the musicians take a bow,
we float out of the hall.
Flanked by two golden,
chattering heads,
I am proud: they flourish
into adulthood;
fingers alight
with their father's gift.
I beam as we walk
along familiar streets,
where their parents
once took
a post-concert stroll,
shared a first kiss.

I Am From

Veronica O'Leary

I am from cooking pans, baking bread and nice hot loaves,
the aroma from my mother making scones.
I am from shoes, leather smells, strong sticky glue and the sound
of my father mending shoes.
I am from roller skates, skipping-rope and hopscotch games.
The laughter from my friends and me is like an echo now.
I am from my vegetable garden: tomatoes, lettuce, parsley, rosemary and thyme.
I am from the sound of my children, laughter, tears, fun and
games.
I am from the universe, part of Him who creates all things.

What my Mother Taught Me: a Memoir

Arnold Thomas Fanning

Before I could cook, before I could even conceive of doing that which would go on to give me great and ongoing joy, comfort, and pleasure, there was this:

A kitchen: a Formica-topped wooden table; underneath it a small boy, a child of no more than four years old or so. He looks out from where he sits in his haven on the stretchers between the table legs, his view circumscribed and abbreviated by the table skirting at his eye level.

What he can see: the doors of the kitchen cupboards, the edge of the kitchen sink, the linoleum flooring, the electric cooker, the appliances on the countertops.

Also: his mother, or rather, parts of his mother, her legs and waist only for the rest of her body and head and face are above the line of his vision, out of sight, the view cut off by the tabletop brushing against the top of his mop-haired head.

His mother bustles back and forth, from table to sink to counter to oven, and makes the sounds he is now able to sort and identify and recognise in his mind: the wooden spoon stirring in the mixing bowl, tapping against the rim to loosen its contents; the sound of the spring of the manual weighing scales; liquids being poured, cooling racks being laid on the tabletop with a clatter, greaseproof paper being torn and folded into baking trays, the oven door swinging open and banging shut. Hot wafts of air flood the room along with the smells of fresh baking as the oven door opens.

There is a brief glimpse from under the table of what has emerged from the oven before it is placed on the tabletop with a bang; for the tray is too hot to hold, hot enough to be felt through the oven gloves his mother wears. A whorl of smoke and steam follows from oven to table before his mother jauntily kicks shut the oven door.

The sounds, smells, sights of baking, all taken in by the boy under the table. He shimmies over and without emerging from his hiding place under the table he places his hand, fingers wriggling, on the surface of the tabletop above him, and waits: a message is being delivered, and he awaits the answer. As he does so, he is grinning and giggling in anticipation of what is to come.

— Oh! cries his mother in mock surprise at this sight: for she has seen this, they have gone through this ritual countless times before. A mouse! It's a little mouse!

The boy grins all the more, chuckles in excitement and glee.

Now, into the wriggling fingers he feels a morsel being placed — a still-hot sample of what has been baked, a piece of bun, or slice, what it is that has just come out of the oven to cool. Among the items his mother regularly produces are almond slices, brandy snaps, fairy cakes, devil's food cake, apple pie, jam tarts, sausage rolls.

The hand grasps the morsel, the sample disappears, is consumed, the boy relishes the flood of flavour, echoes of butter, flour, eggs, rendered to something new by heat and processes he does not comprehend, all the while appreciating the flood of sensation from the freshness of the baking, the smell, the texture also. The hand, the wriggling fingers, return to the tabletop. The boy, overcome now by giggling, clutches his belly, grins widely.

— Oh! A mouse! his mother exclaims once more. A hungry mouse!

The boy chuckles and grins, and waits for the next sample.

And so it continues. Until, one day, the mouse came out from under the table.

And then I began to cook.

Butter-on-first toast
Ingredients: bread, butter
Method: heat a grill until really hot. Spread butter thickly onto both sides of the piece of sliced bread. Toast one side of the buttered bread under the grill until the butter has melted and the bread is beginning to brown and crisp; turn the bread and toast on the other side similarly. Serve immediately, on its own, for breakfast.

Possibly, probably, almost certainly, the first thing I learned to cook by myself, as a very young child; the origins of this recipe lost in time but connected with my sense of my family, for I have never known any other family to eat butter-on-first toast, nor any restaurant to serve it. So I think of it as an indulgence of my family alone, even while I do not know where it was first picked up, nor for how many generations it goes back, nor indeed which side of my family it derives from.

It was eaten as a treat many days for breakfast, alternating, of course, some days with regular toast or fried bread, which my father made by spreading beef dripping left over from the Sunday roast onto bread, and frying it until brown on a frying pan.

Breakfast growing up was a greasy, tasty, fat-filled, crunchy affair.

The book
My mother's cookbook, *A Good Housekeeping Cookery Compendium: Compiled by the Good Housekeeping Institute*, is a large, black-vinyl bound volume containing three separate cookery texts put together by the Good Housekeeping Institute in London and published, in a revised edition, in 1954. This is the book from which I first learned to cook and bake, a good two decades after its date of publication.

Signs of my childhood use of the book are evident throughout; notably, on page 35 of the third book in the volume, *Picture Cake Making*, the page depicting a recipe and photo for 'Walnut Coffee Sandwich', a richly flavoured Victoria sandwich sponge cake. The paper is scarred where it has been stuck together in the past by the detritus of cooking, some unknown ingredient, and subsequently prised apart, tearing the surface, leaving rough white patches where an image should be; while down the centre of the gutter, between the pages, there is a deposit of ancient and long-discoloured flour, an indication of the book's use, a moment captured of when it lay open on the tabletop and I spilled the dry and liquid ingredients on it as I referred to it to bake. As it was my favourite baked item, there were, most likely, many such moments.

The book is of its time: a photo early in the first volume depicts the Good Housekeeping Institute, cited as being located at 'Grosvenor Gardens, S.W.1., London', its staff hard at work; women – for it is all women – sensibly dressed in wool skirts and short-sleeved blouses, some sporting strings of pearls, some aprons, seated at rows of desks writing by longhand while at counters nearby other women cook; presumably this is the task of compiling the recipes, which now form this compendium of cookery books.

Sections in the contents have been underlined in pencil, possibly by my mother, possibly by my childish hand: 'Pastry', 'Cold Sweets', 'Tea-Time Cookery', 'Family Recipes', while the Foreword to one of the books asserts: 'It is hoped that *Good Housekeeping's Basic Cookery* will be of real practical help, both as a reference book for housewives, with limited cookery experience, and as a text book for girls learning to cook.'

Boys don't get a look in here; but the book was indeed a 'real practical help' for this boy growing up as he navigated the world of cooking for the first time.

The volume itself today is long past its prime; its black front cover is tearing loose from the spine, the threads of the binding visible, stitching coming undone, while its inserted colour plates are slowly separating from the book as a whole and are now in danger of being lost.

All values used in the book meanwhile are in imperial: Fahrenheit, pounds, ounces, making it a difficult reference for the contemporary cook, while the bulk of the photography, separate from the colour plates, is rendered in black and white, and has not stood the test of time, but rather gives an air of dullness to the entire enterprise, of stultification and doldrums, placing it and its food firmly in a past no longer relevant to the present.

But, despite its flaws and limitations, I love this book, and all that it represents, what it meant to me, and all that it does mean to me; love it for its ageing, for this is in fact a bridge to the past, to when I learned to cook at my mother's side in that afternoon kitchen all those years ago.

The kitchen
A suburban house built in the 1970s, part of a large housing estate in a suburb of South County Dublin, dominated by the Formica-topped table bounded by four spindle-backed wooden kitchen chairs; on the walls, fitted cabinets in an orange laminate, and on the counters below them an array of appliances accrued over the years to supplement the cooker and the fridge-freezer, which was located in the garage conversion just off the kitchen, through a glass door and down a step. These appliances consisted of a deep-fat fryer, a toaster, a kettle, a Breville sandwich toaster, a liquidiser, a Kenwood food processor, an ancient white enamel electric cake mixer. Up above: a black blooming discoloration from where the oil in the deep-fat fryer caught fire and threw up a plume of smoke and soot and flame in a dramatic explosion that stained the ceiling permanently, no amount of attempted re-paintings making the slightest difference to its presence.

From this kitchen my mother prepared, generally, most of the breakfasts: porridge, French toast, the full Irish. She cooked me lunch during school-term days when I was able to come home on break: home-cut chips, deep-fried sausages, which I slathered with ketchup, salt and malt vinegar.

She also cooked the majority of midweek dinners, although my father handled the Sunday roast. Her repertoire included braised steak, rissoles, Irish stew, casserole, pork and lamb chops, all served, of course, with spuds and veg: cabbage, or parsnip mashed with carrot, or broccoli. This, plus endless baking, baking, baking: cakes, pies and buns, an endless array of rich, filling, flavoursome food constantly emanating from the endlessly hot, steam-filled kitchen.

With all this heavy food being produced by my mother's hands, I do not recall being a particularly thin child, despite my attending the local gymnastics club every Saturday during my primary and early secondary school years. But I was a happily well-fed child.

Walnut coffee sandwich
Ingredients: walnuts, coffee essence, butter or margarine, sugar, eggs, baking powder, milk, flour, coffee butter icing, coffee glacé icing.
Method: cream together the fat and the sugar and beat in the eggs; add the essence, chopped walnuts, flour, a little milk, and baking powder; spread in two greased baking tins; bake at 190°C (375°F) for 25–30 minutes; cool on racks and fill with the coffee butter icing; cover in the glacé icing and decorate with whole walnuts.

More so even than devil's food cake, which my mother often made me as a treat, I loved this rich coffee walnut cake and could never get enough of it. As a child I'd pester my mother to make it for me, which she did frequently, despite the palaver of doing so: not as quick and easy as simply rustling up some jam tarts or fairy cakes, this also involved buttercream and glacé icing and decoration; but I loved it, and she loved to see me happy, and so she would indulge me, often, and make it for me.

Still I wanted more: so she encouraged me to learn to bake it myself, using the Good Housekeeping Institute's *Picture Cake Making* book in the *Compendium* she owned, which seldom left the kitchen. Consequently, walnut coffee sandwiches became my most regular baking endeavour, and I produced them at a prodigious rate during my childhood, from an early age and then throughout adolescence.

I can picture how it must have been when I first began to bake that walnut coffee cake, following the instructions in my mother's cookbook. As a short child, it must have been a struggle to stretch and a challenge to reach up and over the height of that Formica-topped table to measure and weigh and pour and stir the ingredients needed in my mother's large grey delph mixing bowl, and a further delicate procedure to gingerly carry the filled baking trays to the oven. Subsequently, cake baked, it must have been an ordeal to get those hot trays from the torrid oven back to the top of the table and the waiting wire cooling racks without burning myself.

But the pleasure of eating that completed cake, which I consumed more or less all by myself, was the goal and result of all that effort. That was bliss.

Easy béchamel sauce
Ingredients: butter, chopped onion, flour, milk, thyme, bay leaf, whole white peppercorns, grated whole nutmeg.
Method: cook the onion in the butter then add the flour to make a *roux*; gradually add the hot milk and heat through until thickened; add the herbs and spices, cook until flavoured throughout then run through a fine sieve before serving.

Variation: mornay sauce
Add two eggs yolks, cream, butter and cheese (e.g. Cheddar, Swiss cheese, Parmesan).

As a child I took up fishing with great enthusiasm; at a certain point I began to catch fish; and at a certain point after that, late childhood into adolescence, I began to cook the fish I caught; and at a further stage to this still I began to cook the fish I caught with more care, thought, consideration and, finally, sophistication.

I caught pollock, flounder, plaice, codling, gurnard and mackerel from the West Pier at Dun Laoghaire or off the rocks at the sound opposite the island at Dalkey. I would go out early and return late, missing every meal at home in the summer months, arriving home after dark to cook the fish I'd caught that day in a late-night supper for myself.

The simplest of these meals consisted of mackerel fried in butter and served with heavily buttered brown soda bread; a sublime meal, eaten often when the mackerel were running, the fresh fish the best-tasting I ever had. The most elaborate fish meals were when I fried or occasionally poached a white fish such as plaice or pollock and served it with a sauce such as béchamel or mornay.

My family were quite encouraging of these culinary explorations and would take a break from watching TV to come and sample what I had produced that night; the mackerel, by common assent, the fish no more than a few hours out of the sea, the most popular fish supper.

I learned to cook from observing my mother and following what she showed me and developed my cooking from those cookery books I found in my childhood home, not only the *Good Housekeeping Cookery Compendium* but also *The Robert Carrier Cookbook* among others. As life progressed, I never lost my interest in cookery, and over the years developed as a cook, learning new recipes and techniques from a wide variety of food writers such as Darina Allen, Tamasin Day-Lewis, Nigel Slater, Jamie Oliver, Rick Stein, Keith Floyd, Madhur Jaffrey, Ken Hom, Anna Jones, Delia Smith and others, many of whom I watched on TV over the years also.

What I love to cook: fish, particularly tuna, bream, bass and John Dory; Spanish food, remembrance of my time living in Madrid as a young man recently graduated from college, and many subsequent trips to the Iberian peninsula: *tortilla Española, pimientos de padrón, pa amb tomàquet.* My speciality: roast chicken. Also: lamb stew, Cajun blackened fish, pancakes, French toast. Italian food such as marinara sauce, penne with *ragù,* linguine *al tonno,* spaghetti *alla puttanesca,* carbonara, spaghetti *con gamberetti e rucola, insalata caprese.* Further: sweet potato curry, celeriac soup, brownies, scones, the full Irish. And eggs, lots of eggs: fried, boiled, scrambled, poached.

Today cooking is one of those passions that, for me, nourishes not only the body but the mind and soul as well. Furthermore, I love to cook for others: for friends, for family, for my wife. Eating communally with friends or family remains an ongoing source of joy; presenting good food to those who appreciate it is even more fulfilling.

All this joy in cooking derives from my mother, through her encouraging me to cook from an early age. In continuing to cook, I still hold on to a part of her: her memory, her presence, her love, and I carry that love in me, as something vital and essential, to give to others, through cooking.

All this is what my mother taught me, and taught me to be.

In memory: Rose Fanning, homemaker

Sources
A Good Housekeeping Cookery Compendium (Waverley Book Company Ltd, 1952) contains three books in one volume: *Basic Cookery in Pictures, Picture Cookery* and *Picture Cake Making.*
The Robert Carrier Cookbook, Robert Carrier (Sphere Books Ltd, 1970).

Claddagh Ring

Nessa O'Mahony

Two hands, one heart, a coronet,
bought on Shop Street, tied with a bow
for fifty years together. One hand
veined blue, tremoring on his lap
as he learned patience
in corridors and waiting rooms.
The other wore it proudly till
flesh shrank on bone,
the gold loosened.
Their daughter wears it now,
heart inward on the middle finger
to show she's taken, that two hands
grasped hers tightly once, loosely later,
her heart crowned with love.

The Way the Light Falls
(an extract)

Catherine Dunne

Melina: Dublin, February 2017

Let me tell you what I now see around me, Alexia. A closed door. An empty life. Everything is suddenly drained of energy. Even the air is dull and lethargic.

There is a half-full – or half-empty – bottle of wine, left over from dinner earlier. His glass stands on the draining board. Mine is beside it. The red ghosting of my lipstick is still visible around the rim. There it is, for anyone to see: the garish evidence of my sin.

I'm tired and my hands have begun to shake. I need a drink.

I slosh the remainder of the wine into his glass and take it with me, back to the table. Slowly sipping the contents gives me comfort. I can pretend, just for a moment, that he is still here. I can pretend, as I write, that he has just stepped into the bedroom, or outside into the garden for a smoke.

I glance towards the window again. Streetlights bloom in the darkness, a halo of brightness fizzes around the misty, rain-spattered globes. The street is, as far as I can tell, empty. He is not coming back.

I look around for something to distract me, to take my mind off the silence.

There is a patchwork quilt on the back of the sofa. I'd brought it with me here, a few weeks back, to brighten up the stained and sagging cushions. He liked it – but he teased me about my interior designer's horror of our temporary home. Domestic surroundings didn't matter to him in the way they do to me.

The quilt is the one Mama made, after she and Papa returned to live in Cyprus. She'd made one each for you and for me: a kind of symbolic record of our family history, and with it, in a way, the history of Cyprus.

Each square of fabric represents something particular about those who came before us. Here is our Aiya Melina's favourite flower: oleander, pink and luscious and in full bloom. Here's our great-grandfather's farmland, represented by orange groves, their embroidered fruit startling and vibrant against a green background.

Mama whispered a story to me once, about her father's love of the land he'd inherited. He was attached to it as though it was another of his children, she said, and he guarded it ferociously.

Late one autumn, grandfather discovered some pottery in one of his newly tilled fields. Not the shards that he would have expected, remnants of an ancient past that were routinely scattered everywhere, but exquisite bowls, still intact, the blue of their lapis lazuli still gleaming under centuries of dirt, the gold of their rims as perfect as an accusation. Mama remembered watching as her father wrapped them carefully in a blanket, put them into his cart and patted his elderly horse, soothing its restlessness at this sudden change of routine. Before he left, he took his ten-year-old daughter by the shoulders and looked into her eyes. He shook her once, gently. 'Not a word, Phillida,' he said, 'to anyone. Do you understand?'

She nodded wordlessly, but proud nonetheless that her father thought her worthy of a secret, whatever it was. He clambered into the cart then, clicking his tongue, urging his horse into a trot.

'Why'd he do that?' I'd asked her, round-eyed with the childish wonder of buried treasure and family silences.

'He had to hide the bowls, or the government might have taken his land,' Mama whispered, looking around her even then as though something like that could still be possible, all those lost years later, deep in a Dublin suburb. 'Sometimes, people think that preserving things from the past is more important than looking after the living.'

'But that's not fair.' I remember my indignation.

She nodded. 'Life's not fair, Melina. We all have to accept that. And some lives are more unfair than others.'

I run my hand over the soft fabric now, wondering if those ancient bowls still lie, undiscovered, somewhere in the Cypriot countryside. I haven't thought about that conversation in years. I lift one corner of the quilt and see again how somewhere on each square, Mama has sewn, so neatly as to be almost invisible, the names of everyone whose history she could uncover.

She excavated their stories layer by layer, digging into boxes of family photographs, reading letters, journals, even telegrams. In her grandparents' abandoned farmhouse, she came across yellowing sheets of newspaper that lined cupboards, wardrobes, chests of drawers. Their fading print, from time to time, filled in gaps in the extended family narrative.

Either that or they confused her, throwing the received wisdom of events into disarray. But she never gave up. I remember how this act of family archaeology, of reclaiming the past, was one of Mama's pet projects when she and Papa retired to their little house and garden after all the longing years in Dublin. That, and gathering together books of her family recipes. Our mother was so proud of her achievements, proud and fiercely proprietorial. I still miss her.

But it is better that she is no longer with us. Phillida, of the bright smile and the fragrant smells of cinnamon and rose water. Phillida, who loved her garden and her kitchen with an equal passion. Who loved her children above all. Mama.

I run my finger over the square on the quilt that she sewed for me, for what was my life, not so long ago: cerulean blue for the background – blue as the seas around the island I knew so little of until recent years. On the edges, she had sewn a flowering of delicate Cypriot lace.

The lace that Mama used once adorned your wedding dress, Alexia: the one Papa and I hid away from you after what happened, happened. And it bordered the heavy linen tablecloths made by Aiya Melina all those years ago.

It stitched us all together, Irish and Cypriot.

I'm still trying to figure out how I got from there to here. From the days when my naive teenage self helped Papa take all those boxes of memories from the attic to the living room, where they made our mother's face glow.

How did I get from that to this: to my life spiralling away from me, leaving me in some foreign land without a map? When did I stop being able to make myself understood?

How quickly it has all happened.

Rock Pool

Jessica Traynor

Baby, watch the hermit crabs
escape your bucket,
look at the everyday jewels
of their houses –
sand blown to glass.

See them flee from water,
drown in air
like your gasping cries on days
when we fail to meet
your implacable need –

oh periwinkle. Oh limpet.
Oh crab-tango.
Now watch your grandfather,
on days when names
sidestep him in shallows,

tangle in the seaweed of his hair,
drip in the saltwater trail
he traipses through the house.
On bad days, salt crust
on our cheeks.

The world finds its Fibonacci tail;
here are its pincers
                     bearing down,
pinning each beginning to its end.

Remnants

Eamon McGuinness

Frank is sitting at his kitchen table. The radio is on and he is watching the street. In front of him sits a pile of junk mail. His system is simple – let them build up, read, bin or keep. Grainne bought him a 'No Junk Mail' sticker but he took it down and put it in the drawer where he keeps his trinkets. In the summer, when the sun shows up all the dust, she gives the kitchen a proper going over. He smiles to himself, thinking of her picking up the sticker and saying 'Aw, Dad!', or maybe he'll be gone by then and she'll just smile and sigh 'Ahh, Dad.' But for now, he's watching, 'cause Noely always passes at this time and maybe he'll have something for him today. Gustavo won't be around until five.

The kitchen and living room have been converted into one space and the girls had a sit-down shower put in in the back. The parlour is his bedroom now. They bought him a smartphone too. The buttons feel slippery and the images slide off the screen. He's learnt to read what they send him and has his own system to reply. Last week, Gustavo showed him how to use the camera function and took a picture of them together at the kitchen table. Gustavo gripped his left hand onto Frank's shoulder and took the picture with his right.

In his notepad, Frank writes a message for Grainne and Melanie: *Nice day today. No news. Hope all are well. Thanks for yesterday, see you during the week, please God.* He takes a picture of it with one button and with two more clicks it arrives on their phones. Grainne writes back before he has a chance to put the phone away. She always writes something, even if he didn't ask a question – *ta, xxx* or one of those smiley faces. Melanie rings him every evening after dinner. He never throws away a note after he's written it. If he needs to say something longer, he'll ring and talk or leave a voicemail. He's been thinking whether to ask Gustavo for his number. He doesn't think he'd call him or write him a note, but it'd be nice to fill up the contact list all the same.

Noely passes at nine and doesn't stop, look or wave in his direction. The last thing he brought was the electricity bill and a special offer from that hotel in Mullingar. The week before was a Valentine's card from young Beth and that's hanging on the wall now. It's on the little thread of twine over the mantelpiece where the Christmas cards go. Grainne took them down in January, stacked them into a pile and was going to throw them out until Frank stopped her.

'Why do we send them if they just end up thrown out?'

'It's tradition, Dad.'

'I think people should be allowed keep them up as long as they want.'

'You'd look like a mad auld lad if you were found like that.'

He ignored her comment but knew what she was getting at. That bachelor who was found last March in Wexford town, his Christmas lights still blinking and him on the couch as cold as ice with the TV on. A neighbour noticed a holly wreath on the door, looked in the front window and rang the Gardaí. *Maybe that's the best way to go*, Frank thought. *Who wants to go surrounded?*

The important cards get stuck on the fridge: the new dentist on the fifteenth, Dr Sorley on the nineteenth. He wonders what Sorley's receptionist did with the card he sent them in December. He liked being in there before Christmas and seeing it hung up in the waiting room beside the others. The calendar is still in its place. Rory's class made it. Now there's a drawing of a house by Paul Breen in Second Class. Frank knows Rory's picture is July.

He was shown it on Christmas Day but hasn't looked at it since. He'll save it and try to forget about it until 30 June or 1 July and then see if the picture is the same as the one in his head. He remembers a horse with five legs and three eyes and four people on its back and they're riding towards a river. Rory told him the story behind it, but he can't remember. Noely and Gustavo are the cowboys now, riding around the city delivering post in all sorts of weather.

Frank doesn't know why people are so obsessed with throwing things away. He likes remnants. 'Things go at their own time,' he said to the girls a few Sundays back. 'At the beginning of November, you see used fireworks on the grass, in January odd bits of Christmas tree here and there and after an election there's always a stray poster in a field and those plastic things left on the poles. Things will just disappear eventually, of their own accord, without all this fussing and organising.' They didn't know what to say and eventually Grainne changed the subject and started talking about the kids.

Last Friday, Frank told Gustavo about the bedrooms. Maybe he shouldn't have, but Gustavo was talking about the place he rents, and it got Frank angry; sixteen of them in a house, four to a bedroom, two bathrooms, one kitchen and that crook charging them three hundred a month each. Frank had heard all the rent talk, seen the homeless people on the news and it just came out: 'Sure Gustavo, I've two spare bedrooms here, you and a couple of your buddies could move in rent free.' He didn't tell the girls that he said it. Gustavo changed the conversation quick enough. He was drinking tea without milk. He thinks milk in tea is strange. There was a silence and Gustavo broke it by showing Frank where he's from on a map on his phone. He adds a Y to Frank's name for some reason. Franky. He stayed for half an hour and when he was leaving Frank wanted to, but didn't mention, the bedrooms again. He was going to say 'Gustavo, think about it, son, it'd save you a few quid. It would.' But it was late, and Gustavo was rushing and had to get all his leaflets delivered. He told Frank he'd be back around next week and would call into him then.

When he was gone, Frank went through the leaflets and decided to order himself a fish and chips and get it delivered. The delivery lad was wiry, and Frank saw him sprint up the driveway; he left the car running and was hopping from one foot to the other. He called Frank 'sir' and was walking away before Frank could give him a tip. Frank called him back and asked him his name. He told him it was Kyle Quinn.

'That's very modern.'

'Don't ask, I hate it.'

'Frank Murphy is my name, son. Thanks for the chips and have a good night.'

He shook his hand and gave him two euro. He took a picture of the chips with a little note beside it for the girls. Grainne sent back three smiley faces and Melanie rang him before bed to see was he alright.

His sons-in-law aren't half as interested in him as Gustavo is. They were there yesterday in Grainne's and spent most of the time looking at videos on their phones and laughing at things no one else could see. Gustavo should be around soon. He said: 'See you next week, Franky.' He usually comes on Mondays and Fridays around four. Noely is probably having his afternoon nap now. He told Frank once that he loves having a nap before the wife and kids get home. In the end, yesterday, Frank told them about Gustavo, not the bedrooms, but the cups of tea, the map and his visits. They all got angry then, saying he could be this, he could be that and to be careful bringing people into the house. 'Shut up,' Frank said after a while, 'yis don't know him, the lad is just delivering a few leaflets to pay his bills. I needed a bulb changed one day and he did it for me then stayed for a cup of tea. No harm.' He told them about the landlord, the one kitchen, his rent and two jobs. They all looked confused. Melanie asked:

'How does a Mexican get a job in An Post?'

'He's not Mexican,' Frank said, 'and he doesn't work for An Post.'

He got her to get the map up on her screen and showed them where he was from, but they didn't care about Brazil. The lads started talking about Dunga, Ronaldo and Ronaldinho. Frank interrupted them and said, 'There's more to Brazil than football, lads. Their political system is worse than ours. Their president is a crook.' He was just quoting Gustavo. They all nodded and agreed but Frank was glad they didn't ask him any questions, so he didn't have to go into specifics.

The kids are drifting home from school now, kicking bags and punching arms. They all have one earphone in as they chat, and a boy and a girl are sharing a pair. People are walking their dogs. It's a nice evening so Frank pulls his little stool out to the porch and sits there. He brings the radio with him. After an hour, he sees this red-coated figure across the road with a heavy-looking satchel. She's slow and looks to be dragging her feet. The bag seems to be weighing her down. She makes her way to the corner house then crosses and he sees her move along the road. Everyone else has 'No Junk Mail' signs up so it'll be no time before she gets here. She stops at the gate and Frank waves her in.

'C'mon love, what have you got there?'

She takes her earphones out, messes with her phone and looks at Frank as if she has just woken up.

'I have leaflets, do you want?'

'Of course I do.'

She hands them to him with a bit of distance, like Frank's a guard dog who could bite her hand off.

'Thanks love,' he says.

As she's turning around he feels his right leg shaking, the way it does when the girls start talking about nursing homes or him moving in with one of them.

'Excuse me, love?'

'Yes.'

'Where's the other lad?'

'Who?'

'The lad, the man who delivered for the last few weeks, from Brazil.'

'There are many deliverers.'

'Gustavo is his name. Do you know him?'

'Yes, yes, Gustavo is my friend, he gets me this job. He is working full-time now.'

'In the restaurant?'

'Yes, the restaurant.'

She turns to leave and is nearly at the gate when Frank calls again.

'Sorry, love?'

'Yes?'

'Will you tell him I was asking for him?'

'I'm sorry, I don't understand.'

'Could you tell him I said hello?'

'OK, no problem. I will send him a message.'

'He'll remember me. Number thirty-four.'

'OK, thank you.'

She moves away and stops two houses up. She looks around with a confused look on her face, as if she has forgotten where she is and what she is doing. She is looking at her phone and puts one earphone in. Frank walks onto the path, carefully watching his step. He leans on his front gate. All the other noises on the street get louder in his ear and he tries to raise his voice, to carry it up the road, like an alarm or a child's scream. He's not sure if she can hear him but he calls out anyway: 'Frank. Frank Murphy is the name. Franky.'

In the Ruins of the Old Country Church, Somerset

Noel Duffy

I walk across the rubble to where
the door once stood; the wood long stolen
or returned to the soil by the rain
that washes away everything in the end.
Ivy creepers wrap around the half-fallen
stone facade, their embrace melancholic
yet comforting. I enter, the sunlight casts
its light and shadow through the empty
window arches, the pulpit still standing
before the collapsed gable, half shrouded
and hard in its granite making.
I move up the aisle slowly, stop at the figure
of a wild man carved onto a stone arch,
totemic and weird as though looking
from a forgotten past, pagan and untamed,
foliage sprouting from all about his bearded,
almost mocking, face. He is the Green Man
that the old people speak of, come in from
the wildwood to hide in this sacred place
of altar and prayer, the saints and the martyrs
that once lined its walls in alabaster, the long-
forgotten murmur of matins and vespers…

He somehow seems to have outlived it all,
this creature brought in from the cold,
his forest now reclaiming its place here,
a reminding spirit of where we came from
and where we will each return, outlasting
the vaulted, crumbling arches of this old stone church
and the ghosts of its supplicants kneeling in praise.

Once Upon a Time in … Bolivia

Alan McMonagle

I was at the bus station in Sucre, Bolivia. It was early, already warm. Flies kept landing on my head. A smell of rotting meat was making my stomach lurch.

I wanted to buy a ticket to Uyuni, a little over two hundred miles further south and gateway to Salar de Uyuni – the largest salt flat in the world. I had read about Salar de Uyuni when I was very young. Seeing it would fulfil a childhood ambition.

The only other person queuing for a ticket was an old lady. As yet, no one was manning the ticket office. A stack of empty wicker coffins rested to one side of the bus. I was getting worried as, according to the timetable, the bus was due to depart.

'Don't worry,' the old lady said, even though I hadn't expressed a word of concern. 'The bus isn't going anywhere. Not until it is full.'

I turned to her and thanked her. Then I turned around again. Sight of the empty coffins, however, was starting to unnerve me. And so, once again, I turned around to face the old lady.

She was wearing a black bowler hat and matching black poncho. Her face was the colour of leather, a network of dirty fissures scored into her skin from long life and too much sun. She reminded me of one of the women I had seen at the Witches' Market in La Paz. Sure enough – and yet again without a word from me – she confirmed my hunch.

'I have a piece of ground on Calle Linares,' she told me. 'I sell sugar, reading glasses and iPods.'

'How much for an iPod?' I asked her. 'Mine was stolen last week.'

'They are not cheap,' she conceded, 'but my reading glasses are going for a song.'

We stopped speaking. Two backpackers – a man and woman – joined the queue. They'd obviously had an argument recently because they stood side by side, the one looking unhappily away from the other. Another man, squat, horseshoe moustache, and wearing a sombrero – a station employee, I assumed – appeared and loaded two of the coffins into the back of the bus. Though it was hot I shivered.

'You look a little pale,' the old woman said to me. 'Try one of these.' And she offered me the paper bag of coloured sweets she had been holding.

'Thanks,' I said, helping myself.

'*De nada.*'

There was still no sign of a driver. Still no one to man the shuttered ticket office. I reached in my rucksack and took out one of the English-language books I had found at Witches' Market. A pocket-size, hardback copy of *Dubliners*. As soon as she noticed me start to read the old lady nudged me and asked did I need reading glasses.

'No, thank you,' I said.

'Are you sure?' she said. 'I have good reading glasses. No one has ever returned any.'

'I'm fine,' I said, and continued reading where I stood.

Another backpacker joined the queue, a fair-skinned young woman with pigtails and steely blue eyes. A Swede. Perhaps a Norwegian. Another one in search of the salt flats, I assumed. I was about to ask her when the squat man in the sombrero reappeared and loaded another coffin into the bus.

When we spoke to each other again the old woman and myself exchanged reasons for our being at the bus station on this hot morning. I explained my desire to see the salt flats, mentioned youthful reading, my discovery in a book of a twelve-hundred-mile expanse of solid salt. Ever since I was a boy I've wanted to see it, I told her.

The old lady started to chuckle heartily. Bits of the sweet she had been chewing on flew my way. I could see her ravaged, swollen gums. Spittle bubbled in the gaps between her teeth.

'Salt,' she spluttered, while slapping her knee and turning to the others in the queue. 'I have all the sugar in La Paz and this *loco* wants to see salt.'

As she laughed three more backpackers joined the queue, a guy and two women. The women wore singlets and short skirts to show off their tanned though mosquito-bitten arms and legs. The guy was a jittery beanpole of know-it-all chatter. Though he spoke English it was difficult to ascertain where he and his companions might be from. As before, the man in the sombrero reappeared, paused as if to double-check, then loaded three coffins into the bus. The old lady had yet to stop laughing. There was still no sign of the driver.

'How far are you going?' I asked the old lady when her laughter simmered down. She cleared her throat and told me she was travelling to Potosí, a mining town about halfway to Uyuni. She was going to a miner's funeral, she said. It was her first time home in five years.

'Did you know the miner?' I asked her.

'Yes,' she said. 'He was my great-grandson.'

'How old was he?' I asked next, the words were out of my mouth as soon as she'd mentioned her relationship to the dead miner.

'He was twelve. His lamp stopped working and he lost his way. It must have been very dark when he died.'

Again, we stopped speaking. The mosquitoes had, by now, fallen for my blood in a big way. Another backpacker joined the queue. Another coffin was loaded into the bus. I tried returning to the story in *Dubliners* I had been reading, but I couldn't get that image of the boy in the mine out of my head. Over my shoulder I heard her ask again if I needed reading glasses.

Then, what I took to be the bus driver showed up. With one hand he was tucking the shirt of his uniform into his trousers. With the other he was drinking from a glass of clear liquid I was fairly certain was not water. Of course, I could have been mistaken.

'*Madre de Dios*,' the old lady hissed.

'Is there something wrong?' I asked.

'This *loco*. When he drives it is never good.'

'I thought you said you hadn't been this way in five years.'

'Yes, and this *loco* drove us into a ravine.'

A third voice broke in on our conversation. It was one of the trio of backpackers, the know-it-all beanpole.

'Hey, brother,' he said to me a little too loudly for my liking. 'What's with the coffins?'

'Search me,' I said, *and I am not your brother.*

'Every time someone joins the queue, he loads one. Have you noticed?'

'Talk to the old lady,' I said. 'She's been this way before.'

But the old lady had scarpered out of the queue. I looked up and it was then I noticed that the ticket office had opened, and there she was, already making her purchase and then making her way onto the bus where she had the pick of the seats. Suitably encouraged by this favourable turn of events, we all followed suit and purchased our tickets. As did a steadily arriving procession of more backpackers, who turned up individually or in two and threes, happily noted the not-yet departed bus, purchased tickets and piled aboard. Whereupon and without exception sombrero man appeared and loaded the relevant numbers of coffins into the bus.

Two hours later we were still sitting on the bus, waiting for the last remaining seat to be filled, waiting for the driver to fire up his engine and begin the journey south. In this time the old lady and myself had swapped some more talk about La Paz, about the *loco* in charge of today's bus journey, about the reading glasses best suited to the shape of my head. We said nothing more of the boy in the mine and eventually we had run out of things to say. At some point I looked out the window just as the passenger we had all been waiting for – a tiny, middle-aged woman lugging a huge trolley case over the bumpy ground – arrived, waving manically at the bus driver not to leave without her. She needn't have concerned herself. The driver was only too happy to indulge her.

The tiny woman clambered aboard, claimed her seat. Right on cue, our man in the sombrero appeared again, and we all watched as he loaded the last coffin into the bus. Who is going in those? I could sense my fellow travellers wondering, and I looked over to the old lady, but she just smiled vaguely, reluctant, this time, to supply a response to the unspoken concern. And at last the engine growled into life, the driver revved for all he was worth, and gripping the steering wheel with both hands, he swung his quarry out of there, all the time grinning like a let-loose madman.

Love Is a Decision

Paul Perry

I was determined not to be tricked into using words.

He hit me: what do I feel?

I was about to say pain, but said nothingness.

The days went on.
I avoided the others, stopped laughing.

At times, it drove me crazy rattling in my brain not allowed to
think of anything else.

I jump up and throw it out.

Other times, I go down.
Down.
Down with it, down beneath words where my breath is gentle.

It's like looking up through a lake and the surface is a sentence –

what it reads is nothingness.

What it says is love.

Santa Baby

Roisín O'Donnell

Sorry, this is not a very happy story. But it could have been worse.

If I had realised the bells on Rudolf's antlers sat directly over my nipples, I would not have worn that jumper to the school Christmas grotto. I'd bought the jumper without trying it on, not stopping to wonder why it was in the bargain section of Penneys. Then, on the evening of the grotto, I was in such a mad rush, trying to get my girls to the childminder's, before driving the twisting country roads back out to St Brigid's, that I threw the jumper on and didn't even look in the mirror until I was in the staff toilet, ten minutes before *The Star of Christmas* was about to begin. In the harsh light of the naked bulb, I saw my hat hair, dark roots, and the frown lines and shadows under my eyes. I also saw the bright red jumper with its winking reindeer nipple bells and lettering that spelt *hurry down the chimney tonight* in gold sequins. 'Christ,' I whispered. 'Shit.'

'Now Connie,' Patricia said, when I walked into the staff room. She gave me that quick recce glance, which always reminds me why she is the principal. She has this supernatural ability to notice *everything*, at all times. She can spot a teacher in an inappropriately sexy jumper and devise a plan to hide her away while maintaining a magnanimous smile. 'While the plays are going on,' she said, 'I'd like you to stay in the grotto with Santa and take the photos, OK?'

'Sure,' I agreed. Newly arrived up from Dublin, my temporary contract at St Brigid's meant I'd do anything for the chance of permanency. 'Take the photos' sounded like an important job. It was only afterwards I realised the principal wanted me and my jumper hidden out of sight of the hordes of parents currently filtering into the already steamed-up hall, sitting on plastic chairs of various heights to watch *The Star of Christmas*, followed by *The Runaway Reindeer* and *Aliens in Bethlehem*.

If I hadn't been wearing that jumper, Patricia wouldn't have led me into the seductive glimmer of Santa's grotto, in the converted Fourth Class classroom. 'There's the camera,' she said, 'Just point and click. And keep an eye on those elves, there's to be no messing.'

Wearing toe-curled slippers and jester hats, with painted cheeks and dotted freckles, the elves were at the laptop. From the projection on the interactive whiteboard, I could see they were on YouTube, trying to change the cheerful Christmas playlist onto something by Kanye West.

'Yous lot, AWAY FROM THE LAPTOP,' Patricia ordered. 'You're to hand out cookies and bring them children in to see Santa, and there is to be ABSOLUTELY NO MESSING, understand?'

'Yes Mrs Reilly.'

'Now, Connie, just keep an eye on that fire exit. The big man will be arriving soon. I told him to come round the back. Last year when he made an entrance through the hall, there was absolute pandemonium.'

If she hadn't said that, I wouldn't have seen Santa coming up the disabled ramp, the mizzle of the damp December evening clinging to the fake fur of his red velvet suit. A haze of dark trees gathered close around the playing field of the small whitewashed school at the bend of the crossroads. I pushed the bar of the fire exit down, letting in a cold wind, and stood back to let Santa into the cosy nook of the grotto.

'Mrs Daly,' he said, wiping his boots on the snowman mat. 'How are things?' He was a Coca-Cola-ad Santa, with an authentic-looking belly and thick white beard. All I could see were his eyes behind fake half-rim glasses, but I recognised his voice. He had the Meath accent I was getting used to since moving out here, but his was a softer version.

'Micheál. How are you?'

'Not a bother, thanks. This is me here, I take it.' He sat down in the high-backed carver chair and looked up at the twinkling grotto. 'They've done a grand job on the place.'

'It's lovely, isn't it?'

We both looked around at the fairy lights and reindeer posters, the LED lanterns, the red tinsel that shivered in a draft from the fire exit. Santa turned to the elves.

'Well then. How are yous?'

The elves nudged and nodded. At twelve and thirteen, I doubted that these kids still believed in Santa, but they were going along with the charade for our benefit. Then they skipped out of the grotto, their movements coordinated like a shoal of cod, moving in unison. Left alone with Santa by the crackle of the fake fire in its cardboard fireplace, I forced a smile and folded my arms across my chest to hide the jumper.

'So, how are you keeping?' I asked. 'Saoirse did great in her Christmas tests, did she tell you?'

'I heard about that, yes.'

There was a lull. The final crescendo of 'Feed the World' blasted on the sound system. If I had spoken too soon, and hadn't let that awkward pause fill the grotto, perhaps Micheál would not have said anything else. But I was numb from tiredness and suddenly missing my girls. So he spoke again.

'My relationship with Saoirse has taken a nosedive lately, to be honest.' He sat back, lacing his fingers across his belly. 'It took me by surprise. I didn't see it coming.'

'Oh. I'm sorry to hear that,' I said.

'You know, of course, her mam and I are separated. Saoirse blames me for leaving. There's a lot of anger, and she's a right to be angry.'

The track had changed. '*I don't want a lot for Christmas,*' Mariah Carey was warbling. My throat felt tight. I wished the bloody elves would skip back in here.

'It's hard,' Micheál continued, 'the emotional and verbal stuff. When you've not a bruise to show for it. I sometimes think if Martina had beat me black and blue, it'd be easier to explain. But it's the emotional stuff. And she's doing it to Saoirse now. Silent treatment. Criticising. Controlling. It's hard to watch. When it's your child.'

It was hot in the grotto. I wanted to take my itchy jumper off. 'Saoirse's a great girl,' I said. 'If you just give her time.'

'Ah well, it's just … now I'm not living with her, I don't have the same influence.' He sat back, hidden behind his beard and wig. 'I've lost her. That's the truth of it, Mrs Daly, if you'll excuse me for being dramatic. I've lost Saoirse, and it's tough. Just doesn't feel like an awful lot to live for at the moment. But look it … sure you don't want to listen to me prattling on here. How are you settling in?'

If I had been a bit braver, I might have told him I knew exactly what he was talking about. I'm not sure what stopped me. Perhaps it was the fear that if I started to tell my story, it might have pumped out of me, unstoppable. Like blood from a stab wound. As it was, the first child rang the doorbell to see Santa.

'Are yous ready?' one of the elves hollered, and the cohort of them stampeded back into the grotto, bells jingling.

Micheál fell into role, greeting a star-struck shepherd with a checked tea towel on his head, 'Hello there. Who have we here?'

I ducked behind the camera and spent the next three hours snapping family cameos. There was the toddler who wandered into the grotto, took a look at Santa and stumbled three steps back, the parents who pretended they didn't want to be in the photo, and then the Instafather who dived straight in, 'Let's get a photo with Dad,' planting a kiss on the cheek of his embarrassed ten-year-old. There were three brothers scowling up, having recently had a fallout, and there was a steady parade of shepherds, kings, angels, aliens. I felt like I was drowning in the sweet, rich, melancholic claustrophobia of Christmas.

'Speed this up!' Patricia ducked her head into the grotto at around seven. 'Come on Santa, we've to wind this up soon.'

As the queue dwindled, I tried to think of something to say to Micheál. Click, click, click. Family after family paraded in front of us. I thought of my own kids, knowing this time next year, the cameo would be shattered. If I had the strength to follow through.

'All done.' Micheál stood up.

My flight instinct took over. I shook his white-gloved hand. 'Happy Christmas, Micheál, and have a lovely New Year.'

'You too, Mrs Daly. You too.'

Cursing myself for not having said more, I ducked out of the grotto, picked up my bag and coat and dashed out into the dark, rainy night.

*

If I hadn't arrived home so late, my girls would not have been crying and my husband would not have been fixing me with stares that could have been bottled and labelled *Pure Hate*. 'How was your evening?' I asked.

'Alright. You?'

'Fine.' I swallowed and felt stories and conversations dissipate into the gloom. If it hadn't been for my conversation with Micheál, I might not have been able to keep smiling through bath and bedtime, feigning ignorance of my husband's murky silence. If I hadn't been thinking about Micheál and Saoirse, I wouldn't have held my one-year-old daughter tight against my chest in the dark, her chubby cheek on my bare shoulder, feeling the weight of her warmth and letting hot tears slide down my face. 'So, it's the loss of the love?' my therapist had asked at the last session. 'Despite the abuse he puts you through, that's what's holding you back. The memory of love.' I fell asleep in the rocking chair in the baby's bedroom, my reindeer jumper gathered in her chubby fist.

*

Waking, my eyes felt hot. But it also felt as if something had been cleansed and washed away. If I hadn't cried that night and felt the tension melt, I might not have decided to make a left turn on my drive home from school the next day. I might not have driven down bumpy country roads, through a tunnel of bare branches, following a map from my memory of our class visit to Micheál's farm last September. I took another left and followed the laneway over potholes filled with puddles that reflected the white winter sky. I remembered Saoirse helping her dad out in the milking parlour that day, the spatter of violent green cow shit, the chug of the warm milk as it sloshed into the canisters, and the puffs of the stamping Friesians' warm breath as the class of kids crowded round to watch.

The school trip had been part of a project on modern farming techniques. If it hadn't been for that visit, I wouldn't have known where Micheál lived. I wouldn't have driven up that rocky lane and parked outside a barn with a rusting tin roof and a row of cows chewing quizzically at me. I wouldn't have stepped out of the car with a hastily written Christmas card in my hand.

'Mrs Daly?' In the doorway, Micheál looked naked without the fluffy camouflage of his white beard. So the Santa belly had been padding. My cheeks burned. For a second, I worried that this would be like two strangers meeting up after a one-night stand, finding that whatever spark of connection they had imagined under strobe lighting has dissipated in the daylight.

'I brought you a Christmas card,' I said, proffering it stupidly.

(I know, this is not a happy story but it could have been so much worse.)

The cows were lowing. Winter hedgerows were a purple haze in the gathering dusk. Micheál took the Christmas card and smiled. 'That's very kind. Will you come in for a cup of tea?' he said.

Swing

Kate Dempsey

This automatic muscle memory
has you tilting back, legs outstretched,
hands grip the knobby chains,
the warm smell of steel clings to the skin,
the clunk and squeal of the unstable frame,
head back, hair streaming,
stomach left below.

This pause, this breath-stopping hang,
you want it to last,
to kick your shoes over the stone parapet
between the swing park and the worrisome world

and finally, let go,
release to arc up and beyond,
soar into the quiet sky,
escape gravity, leave every petty thing behind
to pierce the thin blue line,
that precious sphere
which shields our fragile lives.

Feeling Savage
(an extract)

Madeleine D'Arcy

Mags Phelan – 1979

Mags is sitting behind the cash desk in Belinda's Boutique, watching the clock. It's a quarter past five and she's dying to go home. There are no customers. The place is driving her out of her mind. She feels like an eighty-year-old but she's only nineteen. Well, truth be told, she's sixteen but she's been lying about her age so long she's almost come to believe she's nineteen herself.

Belinda's Boutique has nothing in it she'd ever want to buy. There's no Belinda, just Mrs Mackey, a corseted glamour puss with bad teeth. Thirty quid a week is all she pays Mags for sitting in a godawful shop that smells of cheap air freshener, pretending the clothes look good on the few women who come in to try them on and putting up with Tracey, the other shop assistant. There are no perks of the job either. Mrs Mackey is so mean she closed the shop for a day when Pope John Paul II visited Ireland earlier in the year and trotted off with her husband to Galway to see him, but she made Mags work an extra day the following week to make up for the day off. She'd given Mags the job without asking for references or even asking how old she was. If Mags had been asked, she'd have had to lie.

In Belinda's Boutique, a dusty radio/tape recorder sits on a shelf below the cash register. Mrs Mackey's told them they can listen to RTÉ Radio 2 or else play the easy-listening cassette tapes she's chosen for the shop: Phil Coulter, Acker Bilk and the like. Mags has a few decent mixtapes hidden in a drawer – Elvis Costello, The Ramones, The Undertones – but Tracey is forever switching off her tapes and turning on the radio instead. RTÉ radio only plays awful rubbish like Olivia Newton-John, Cliff Richard and Irish country and western, and it's nearly as bad as the easy-listening tapes. The more time Mags has to spend in this shop, the more she hates it. Mags can't even sit on the crummy staff toilet now because Tracey told her last week that she was suffering from genital warts. Tracey is an utter slag, even though she still goes to mass, and her taste in music is horrendous. Tracey is someone whose guts Mags feels she can legitimately hate, although she doesn't have to have legitimate reasons to hate people. She hates Tara, her housemate, as well, because Tara's so fucking nice it drives her crazy.

Anyway, this, like so many other situations that Mags has found herself in since she left home a year ago, is only a temporary one. Mags is saving up for her escape, which is difficult on her pissy little wage, for sure, but someday soon, she'll get away. It's unfortunate that it's taking longer than she'd hoped because she keeps having to buy more clothes and spend money on essentials like going to the Paradise Club every Saturday night. Without the Paradise Club to look forward to, though, she'd never be able to manage the rest of the week.

Mags turns off the radio and shoves a mix tape in the cassette player. Elvis Costello, 'Watching the Detectives', and she turns it up loud.

Tracey protests. 'You know Mrs Mackey says ...'

'If you don't shut up, I'll tell Mackey about the warts on your cunt,' says Mags, and dances around the shop floor until the clock shows five-thirty on the dot.

*

The small crooked house that Mags shares with Tara is one of a row of badly built old houses that strain against each other on the side of a hill. They might as well be living on top of a mountain, Mags often thinks, the way the wind curls through the faulty window frames and around the edges of the doors. To keep warm, she has three choices: wear lots of clothes; put up with the life-threatening fumes of an old oil heater; or light the gas oven in the kitchen and leave the oven door open.

It's a bitter cold winter and Mags has been drinking gallons of cocoa. There's something about the warm chocolatey smell that comforts her. The house is so lopsided that when she puts a saucepan of milk on the ancient New World stove it looks as if the milk will pour itself straight back out again and so it boils over often. When it does, her heart sinks at the thought of scrubbing the flaky milk skin off the elderly hob yet again.

Mags spends a lot of time handwashing her clothes. Her hands are getting sore from it, so she bought hand lotion for the first time recently – Atrixo, with a lemony smell – but it reminded her of her mother, so she put it away and bought a pair of Marigold rubber gloves instead. She spends a lot of time ironing, too. It's like a disease, this constant washing and ironing. There's no wardrobe in her bedroom so Mags has screwed hooks on every spare bit of wall, and a few in the ceiling, to put hangers on. Everything except the clothes she's wearing is swaying on those hooks. Everything, including her scarves, floats around the room. She'd never admit it to anyone but it's beginning to freak her out. The room looks as if a lot of people have hanged themselves in it.

She's determined to create the perfect wardrobe on very little money. She's planning to leave at short notice as soon as she has enough cash, and when she does, she doesn't want to be caught on the hop. She's going to just slide her clothes into her suitcase and run to her future life.

*

It's so cold this evening that Mags practically runs all the way back to Dominick Street but she's still frozen to the bone by the time she reaches the crooked house. She unlocks the front door and breezes into the kitchen, propelled by a gust of icy wind so strong she has to shove the door closed against it.

A cold sausage lies in the frying pan on top of the old hob, stuck in a pool of grease-white fat, but though Mags is hungry it doesn't look appealing. Instead, she puts milk in a saucepan and while she waits for it to heat, she finds her mug and dumps a spoonful of cocoa powder into it.

Then she hears a knock on the door, followed by the clattering of the letterbox. She has a good mind to pretend she isn't in. It's not the first time Tara has locked herself out, but that's usually at night, after the pub. Tara suggested hanging a key off a string so you could pull it through the letterbox but Mags said it wasn't safe so they hadn't. Mags darts the few steps to the door and opens it, saying, 'Fuck sake Tara, don't say you've lost your keys again …' as she dashes back to save the milk – but it's already boiling over, so she grabs the saucepan off the hob and puts it in the sink and curses.

'Mags. Long time, no see,' says a man's voice, and her heart sinks.

Barry Pattmore has stepped into the kitchen, and as Mags turns, he pushes the door closed behind him.

The old fart stands there, with the same round babyish face, heavy-lidded eyes and calm lizardy smile she knows so well. His big tweed coat is open, despite the cold, and his navy V-neck jumper stretches tight round his belly above his brown corduroy trousers. Mags has never seen him wear anything else but brown elephant cords except for the blue three-piece suit he wears to work. She hasn't seen him since she left home more than a year ago, and his voice is still as calm as it had been then, in the background of her mother's screeching.

'What are you doing here?' Mags asks. Cork is way too small. She should have known he'd find out where she lived sooner or later.

'Your poor mother wants to know are you all right.' Butter wouldn't melt in his mouth. Anyone who doesn't know him would believe his concern to be real.

Xanadu

Colin Dardis

I wish I had longer (we all do)
to create for you a Xanadu.

Some cultures photograph their dead,
Victorian children propped up
alongside their siblings in a pose
only mannequins know;

the artist sketching her mother in a deathbed,
rigor mortis tightening in graphite,
the slack jaw of death falling down the page,
a make-up no mortician could achieve.

Father, I did neither. No photograph, no sketch.
Instead, the best I could do was to fingernail
a fleck of wood off the underside of your coffin,
wrap it in tissue, wish I had taken a thread of lining too.

The Forbidden City

Mary Morrissy

Bernard is sitting at Gate 6D in the departures hall at Abu Dhabi, with two hours to spare after the first leg of his journey east. He is so tired that if he falls asleep, which he knows he will – even on these hard chairs with the metal arms digging into his girth – nothing will wake him. There are no public announcements so he can't even depend on a booming PA to rouse him. It is 3 a.m. for him, but mid-morning here. What to do for two hours? *Coffee*, he thinks. Proper coffee. Not food – he has done nothing but graze from aluminium dog trays for the past nine hours with his knees up around his ears. He needs caffeine – a tub of it.

There's a ground attendant at the counter who has just bundled the last passengers on to a flight to Khartoum – an Indian family, parents, three children and their cling-film-wrapped luggage. He sees she is about to close the gate so he hauls himself out of the bucket seat and pads up to her. Her back is turned. He taps her gently on the upper arm. She stops, turns, flinches when she sees him. *Oh God*, he thinks, *is touching a woman in public a transgression here?*

But he doesn't get outrage from her, just the full force of her vibrancy. Nutmeg skin set off by a slash of vermillion lipstick. There's a name tag pinned to her lapel – *Amal*. He thinks of George Clooney who Olivia used to say she was holding out for when her husband left her. Then George's Amal came along and dashed Olivia's hopes. This Amal is wearing a western-style

111

uniform, a tight rust-coloured skirt, a trim jacket in olive green. Swathed around her neck is a veil that emanates from her head gear, a scarf and hat combined. East meets West.

He feels like a whale in her presence, in the loud Hawaiian shirt he chose for coolness. What a laugh! His pale skin is flushed with the misted residue of old sweat. There are pools under his armpits, plus all the discomforts she cannot see – the chafing thighs, the sweat of his loins.

'You speak English?' he asks, cursing himself for sounding pidginy.

She nods minimally. Bored? Superior? Or afraid to crack her make-up?

'A little,' she concedes.

'I'm looking for coffee,' he says, 'is there somewhere near the gates or do I have to go back?' He points to the maze of brightly lit, duty-free outlets that he has passed without interest. There is no one in his life to buy for – except Olivia, and that's a gift that will have to be chosen with the utmost deliberation, as with all his dealings with her.

'Fat white,' she says, pointing a finger straight at him. It is said with so little inflection that he cannot believe what he has heard. The heat has made him slow-witted.

'I beg your pardon?'

'Fat white,' she repeats, still pointing.

Oh God, is she one of these #MeToo women who's going to make an example of him? Or maybe that's just what she sees. A pasty, pudgy 52-year-old man.

Trip of a lifetime, he told his colleagues when his long-service leave came up. Always wanted to see the Forbidden City. Chinks, they said to him, the chinks have taken over the world, why would you want to go there? (When he was packing, he realised they were right – half of his shirts had *Made in China* labels).

'Communists in capitalist clothing,' Olivia said, 'the most dangerous kind.'

Olivia had been a bit of a politico in her youth, which he remembers, having nursed a low-lying passion for her. But he had done nothing about it, because he knew she didn't see him that way. Very few people saw Bernard that way. He and Olivia started on the same day at City Hall, did orientation together and ended up in Rates. They're the only original ones left, the folk memory of the organisation is how their department head puts it.

'As if we're a pair of doddery old fiddle players with all the tunes in our heads,' Olivia says.

'Or clog dancers,' Bernard adds. (Olivia has recently taken up ballroom.)

She fists him playfully on the arm. Their tenderness is expressed like this, roughly, like a pair of tomboys. She wasn't playful about China.

'Terrible human rights record,' Olivia prodded, 'remember Tiananmen Square? What about Ai Weiwei?' That's Olivia's job – to be the voice of his conscience.

He looks at Amal again as if she has repeated Olivia's impassioned accusations. But there is nothing but indifference in her mask-like face. He feels a tide of fury rising.

'What did you say …?'

'Fat white,' she says evenly.

So that's it, he thinks, I am here to be insulted. Openly. A middle-aged white man who has no finer feelings, the butt of everyone's contempt. Is this how it will be on his guided bus tour of the Great Wall? Except the Chinese won't say it. Not like this. Inscrutable, isn't that how they're supposed to be? But they'll be thinking it, Bernard is sure.

Then, patiently – as if he were infirm – Amal catches his elbow and steers him around to face in the opposite direction, still pointing her finger. She smiles now. It stings, adding insult to injury. Then he sees it. A sandwich board advertising a coffee shop. *Flat White*.

Oh, relief!

He could kiss her, but he won't, of course.

He turns to say thanks but she is gone, strutting off on rust-coloured heels. *All a mistake*, he thinks, *a linguistic misunderstanding. You're tired, you're jet-lagged.* But it is no good. No matter how much he self-consoles, the trip of a lifetime, that precious balloon of escape he has been nurturing so carefully all his life, shrivels, all the air gone out of it. What was he thinking? There is no escape from the body's stubborn armour.

Trimming the Ivy

Mary O'Donnell

My beloved, when I asked him
to trim the ivy on the house,
in his zeal forgot to stop.
Now the house is naked,
her white chest exposed.
Perhaps it's better
to see her skin and bone,
the long tendrils of a plant
in death, brown-veined
while medicinal wind
makes ready
her wintry finery.

Mummy's Christmas Star

Emma Hannigan

Veronique Miller had waited nine years, two months and three days to have a baby. Then suddenly pregnancy was confirmed.

'Are you alright, love?' Derik asked his ashen-faced Veronique. 'Did you hear what the doctor said? We're having a baby!'

Veronique sat perfectly still, staring at the wall in total silence for the longest time. Paralysed by emotion that her dream was finally becoming a reality, she felt utterly overcome. Derik had to lead her by the elbow from the surgery.

The day the baby was born Veronique was a trooper. She endured fifteen hours of labour and only took a few puffs of gas and air.

'I want the full experience,' she managed to utter between contractions. As her face turned an alarming shade of violet and her eyes bulged, Derik wished it was still the 1950s where fathers waited with a cigar poised to be told the good news on the other end of the phone.

'Good girl yourself,' he said shakily as a scene akin to the worst horror movie he'd ever watched unfolded.

When they handed him his son, swaddled in a blanket, with soft peachy skin and a shock of dark hair just like his own, all the previous trials and tribulations melted away. None of it mattered any longer.

'He's perfect,' he said as he sobbed. 'Look at me bawling like a little little girl.' He grinned.

'Isn't he just beautiful, Derik?' Veronique asked proudly. 'And he's all ours.'

Bentley Derik Miller was christened a month later. Every family member, friend, neighbour and colleague they'd ever encountered came along to help them celebrate.

*

Books were a massive influence on Veronique's mothering skills. When she wasn't tending to Bentley she was reading how best to do so.

'Cow's milk has larger molecules of fat, which the body finds more difficult to digest than goat's. Anything containing dairy is now barred from this house,' she instructed Derik when weaning time came around.

Derik had taken up DIY as a hobby to replace long hours on the golf course away from his son – as a result he now owned a shed that was so impressively decked out, most people would happily live in it.

Unbeknown to his wife he installed a small fridge out there, filled with chocolate yoghurts and cream cakes. He figured they tasted even better because they were forbidden.

By the time Bentley was ready to start Montessori, Veronique had researched and visited all the schools in the area. Satisfied she'd chosen the crème de la crème of establishments, she eagerly awaited his first day.

*

Veronique knew it was outstanding that Bentley could read almost fluently, play pitch-perfect Suzuki-method violin, swim like a little fish and speak more French than his father. But she felt the time and effort she'd invested in their son would stand to him.

Several weeks passed by and when Ms O'Neill, the Montessori teacher, sent a note home in Bentley's school bag that November asking for volunteers to help with the nativity play, Veronique felt a warm glow inside. This would be right up her alley.

'I've filled in the form and signed it in the correct place of course,' Veronique told Ms O'Neill the following day. 'But I wanted to make certain you understand I did intend ticking *all* the boxes. I can help with costumes, baking for the after-show.'

*

'So, who's playing Mary?' Veronique asked, cutting to the chase.

'That'll be my Bethany,' Anna said proudly.

'And before there's any sniff of a row,' Macy cut in, 'My Simon is being Joseph! Correct, Ms O'Neill?'

Veronique's head nearly revolved 360 degrees on her shoulders. 'Why?' she spat, forgetting her usual polite decorum.

'Yes, I promised Macy I'd let Simon be Joseph this year. In fairness she's helped out at three previous nativity plays where all her boys have been cattle. So fair is fair, Simon gets the starring role.'

'That hardly seems fair at all,' Veronique said. 'Surely it should be decided by the acting ability of the child?'

'Ah, they're only three, Veronique,' Anna said condescendingly. 'Unless we've a new Macaulay Culkin in our midst, I reckon they're all pretty much the same.'

'Well, as it happens, Bentley has been at stage school on a Saturday since September. I know I might be a teensy-weensy bit biased, but I think he's exceptional. Even if I say so myself.'

'I'm sure he's a marvel,' Ms O'Neill said, 'so we'll give him a little speaking part. How about he can be the first innkeeper Mary and Joseph come to? He can do the whole no-room-at-the-inn thing. That part requires quite a bit of conviction.'

'And he'd have to act like a horrible person,' Anna said with a twinkle in her eye.

'Which won't come a bit naturally to him,' Macy deadpanned.

'Right,' Veronique said, looking furious. 'If that's his part, so be it.'

She went home that day via the haberdashery store and picked up some cream linen fabric and a length of gold braiding. If her son was going to be an innkeeper, she was going to design the most stunning costume for him.

It took a week and every bit of spare time Veronique could shoehorn in between violin, piano, swimming, drama, karate, athletics and horse riding, but she managed to fashion him a striking tunic with matching headdress.

'Wow,' Ms O'Neill said in astonishment. 'With all the gold braiding I think this would be more suited to one of the wise kings,' she mused.

'Oh no,' Veronique snapped. 'This has been made to measure for Bentley.'

'Right then,' the teacher said uneasily. 'Would you be so kind as to make the angel costume also? Macy has used an old rug to make the missing sheep. We've sourced a brown felt donkey from the year before last. Mary and Joseph are sorted too,' she said, ticking off her list.

As December dawned and the excitement of Christmas began to creep in, Ms O'Neill had a little announcement to make as the parents came for pick-up one Friday.

'Rehearsals will get underway from Monday. I have the costumes here and I hope this year's nativity play will be the best one ever!' she said, handing out slips of paper with the children's parts and lines neatly typed out.

Simon grinned from ear to ear and jumped up, punching the air, as he was told he could be Joseph.

'I want to be Joseph!' Bentley yelled rudely.

'Bentley! Stop that!' Veronique said, flushing with embarrassment. 'Wait until you hear who Ms O'Neill wants you to be,' she added, praying he'd calm down.

'Yes Bentley, you're going to be the first innkeeper!' Ms O'Neill announced.

'I won't!' he shouted, folding his arms and pouting. 'I want to be Joseph. Smelly Simon can be the stupid innkeeper.'

'Now, Bentley darling,' Veronique said, bending down to take her son in her arms. 'We must have a little chat about shouting and general behaviour,' she added slowly and clearly. 'Mummy wants you to listen while I explain things. Each year, Ms O'Neill decides who will do what. This year she has thought it all through carefully and she has made her choices.'

'I HATE her choices,' he said, wriggling free of his mother so he could roll on the floor and kick his legs. 'I want to be Joseph!' He burst into hot, frustrated tears.

'Sorry about this everyone,' Veronique said, looking up at the disapproving gazes of the other mothers. 'Once I explain this concept, Bentley will understand. Children only become unreasonable like this when they are threatened and confused,' she added in a knowing manner. She turned to her son. 'Say goodbye to Ms O'Neill properly and tell her you're sorry for getting so upset.'

'No,' he pouted.

'Bentley, sweetie, the reason we must always do our best to be polite is this …'

'OK. Sorry. Bye,' he grumbled.

'Bye, Bentley,' Ms O'Neill said wearily. 'See you on Monday.'

*

Things became fraught once again, however, when Veronique produced Bentley's lines.

'When Mary and Joseph come to your inn,' she explained, 'Joseph will say, "Is there any room at the inn? My wife is having a baby and we've no place to stay." You're meant to pretend to be rather mean and nasty, so put on a cross voice and say, "No, I don't have any room. Now move away." Do you get that?'

'I still want to be Joseph!' Bentley said, bursting into tears.

'That's enough of that now, son,' Derik began. 'You're the innkeeper, so get with the plot.'

'Derik!' Veronique chided crossly. 'Talk the problem through, remember? Explain about others' feelings and how his negative actions may affect them,' she warned in a hushed tone, through gritted teeth.

'Are you sure about all this, Veronique?' Derik asked, looking doubtful. 'In my day, if I talked to my parents like that I'd get a clip around the ear or a smack on the arse. That was the end of it.'

'Times have moved on since that kind of brutal treatment of children was deemed acceptable,' Veronique said, closing her eyes to block out such an image. 'Young people today are nurtured and encouraged. It's so much healthier and more positive.'

'Well, it did me no harm,' Derik said, 'but I'll go along with whatever you say. I'll leave you to it. I'll be in the shed.' Veronique hadn't noticed the black cable running from the house to Derik's shed. She'd no idea he had a reclining leather chair and flat-screen television to keep the fridge company out there.

'Please just work with me for a few more minutes, Bentley,' she begged.

'I don't want to do any more lines,' Bentley sighed, looking glazed. 'I want to watch *Ben 10*.'

'You can watch half an hour of television,' Veronique promised. 'But only once you've shown me you're going to comply with Ms O'Neill and be a good innkeeper.'

'I don't want to be the stupid …' Bentley stopped in his tracks. A sense of calm prevailed and his expression changed. 'OK, Mummy,' he said sweetly. 'I'll be the innkeeper.'

'Good boy!' Veronique said, clapping. 'You're such a wonderful child. I'm so proud of you!'

*

On the day of the show all the parents filed into the school hall. Veronique, Anna and Macy helped Ms O'Neill with the make-up and ensured all the children were dressed correctly in their costumes.

The lights dimmed and the excitement was palpable as the tiny tots' nativity play got underway. All the parents and grandparents wiped tears of pride and joy as their little dotes made their appearances.

Veronique and Derik felt like they'd burst, such was the emotion that washed over them when Bentley took to the stage. The cardboard door worked like a dream as Joseph knocked three times.

'What do you want? Why are you bothering me?' Bentley asked crossly as he answered the door.

Veronique looked over at Derik, glassy eyes brimming with pride. 'Isn't he brilliant?' she managed.

'Amazing,' Derik agreed, shaking his head in awe.

In a monotone voice little Simon, dressed in his Joseph costume deadpanned, 'Is there any room at the inn? My wife is having a baby and we've no place to stay.'

As Mary and Joseph prepared to move to the next door, Bentley stood forward, opened his arms out wide and spoke cheerfully and clearly. 'Yes, I have a beautiful suite overlooking the mountains. You and Mary are very welcome. Come in ...'

The last thing Veronique heard before she fainted from shock was the raucous laughter ringing out in the school hall.

Ways of Seeing the Moon

Breda Wall Ryan

As cross-sawn pine trunk,
as a lantern caught in a tree fork,

as many-eyed lumpen potato,
as leery man-at-the-window,

as new-minted coin,
as mystery, mirror, spy,

as shadowed colony,
as a porthole on night,

as blackness, as an act of faith,
as new and invisible,

as dark light,
as cold shadow-caster,

as magnet,
as midwife of tides,

as once-in-a-season blue,
as goddess in her maiden phase,

as blood sister, rocker of cradles,
as a drowned face in a well,

as split-lipped hare,
as night-lit sky-mushroom,

as ghost of the sun,
as the gleam in the wolf's eye,

as untethered balloon,
as Moon.

Something

Órla Foyle

He drove fast, one elbow out the driver's window, his jacket off and his shirtsleeves rolled up. Her eyes were closed and she was dreaming of adventure. He began to smoke as he steered the car towards Carrauntoohil. She opened her eyes and gazed across his arms to the sea at the edge of the cliffs. The sky had peeled itself back to its original colour; a blue so pale that it was almost invisible.

'I can see the moon,' she said.

He didn't look. The grass verge dipped and cornered against the car.

'Jesus,' he whispered.

She rested her hand on the back of his neck. His neat hair bristled into her fingertips. The car bumped and went faster. It passed stone walls. She rose a little to watch the sea. She wasn't all that sure about the honeymoon. It made her sick, all this love.

He drove fast. His knuckles gripped the steering wheel but now and again they released, and the palm of his hand arabesqued into a left-hand corner turn.

The sea blistered with white sun. *A liquid desert*, she thought. Then she said, 'I could paint that.' She leaned her face against his shoulder. 'If we'd honeymooned in Paris, I could have shown you Monet's gardens.'

He looked at her and she saw something in his face. 'Well at least I got you away from your family,' he said.

Something in his face. Something new that made her cold.

She sat back in the wine leather seat. This was her father's car. Her new husband was driving her father's car. It was a temporary wedding present. See Ireland before you see Africa, her father had joked. She rubbed her halfways fringe from her forehead. Her stomach crinkled on the inside. She was afraid of nothing. She was completely afraid. The middle line of the road bumped underneath the car. Her husband's fingers gripped the gear hard and wrong. 'Soothe it back,' she told him.

And he had looked at her as if he hated her.

She sat back into her seat and a slight, unrecognisable fear sat with her. Her vison blurred and pain tightened in her left eye, yet she focused on the middle line of the road. She wanted to grasp it and fly back with it to the very edge of the morning or even to the previous night. What had she done wrong? What had she missed? She thought of her room upstairs. Its desk, its books and its pencils, and faces and heads drawn on backs of brown paper bags from the shop. Socrates and Beckett.

She tried to see something she had not seen before but she could not see it and after a while, she decided that she had imagined it. It was tiredness. It was relief. It was a headache. It was nothing. This was the start of her honeymoon. It was nothing.

*

Later she almost drowned off the Isle of Capri. It had been a surprise to almost die. A shock of sunny water and her lungs burned bright hot in her chest. She walked back to the beach and her husband was there, seated at an umbrellaed table with another couple. She stood, dripping, in their vision. Her husband offered her a Coke. Everything was quiet in her head. She was still on her honeymoon and she knew she had made a mistake. The world crawled around her. People in other lives. She drank her Coke and sat opposite the other newly married couple. Also Irish and it had been Christopher's idea to pal up with them. Greta's head split with sounds and colours. Her husband wore his black glasses. The other honeymoon couple were delighted with the view of the sea.

The sea was flat, Greta thought. Flat like her husband's face.

*

In Rome, he hit her. A crack across the face in the Capo d'Africa pensione.

'Christopher, let's have a day to only ourselves.'

He hit her then and as she patted her bruises with cold water, she studied her marriage from the corner of her eye. Her marriage was a mistake. She pressed the edges of her bruise then applied make-up until it almost disappeared. Things looked good when they could disappear. She breathed in and smiled and when she went out into the bedroom, Christopher was very sorry. He nearly cried. He said it was the sun heating up his brain.

'Maybe we should forget Africa, then,' she said.

He swallowed as he looked at her.

'We could try somewhere else,' she added.

*

Africa had been her idea. That continent like a club you could hold in your hand. She liked the imagined feel of it. The roughness of its coastline against the edges of her fingers. She touched her bruise.

'You look fine,' Christopher said. He looked pleased.

Another idea had been New Zealand or even Canada but Christopher wanted Africa once he realised how far it slipped down the globe. He was delighted at the deserts and the misleading thin rim of jungles. He heard a priest talk at mass about Nigeria. He told Greta that Africa was where he wanted to go as well. Two years. Two years of giving yourself in the service of others.

There was something in the way he said that. Something that Greta noticed as a small lie but she told herself that it didn't matter. Her stomach was hungry for something she could not actually see. Adventure, she decided. She packed her art things, her books and her clothes. Her sister Jessie watched her from the corner of her bed.

'I don't think he's good,' she said.

Greta fixed on a hat, then pulled her fringe out from underneath the brim. She was going to live in this marriage, she decided. Jessie snorted an angry laugh. She looked mean sitting on the corner of her bed.

'You'll see I'm right, Greta.' She held out her arm. 'He loves giving Chinese burns.'

*

Later in Rome Greta had practised. *Christopher, I need new sandals because my toes are hot and tight in my shoes.*

He almost bought them for her.

The shoe salesman sat on his haunches and lifted Greta's foot to ease the sandal over it, but he could not tighten it over her high arches. He shoved and stretched the raffia strap to the very tip of the buckle. Greta watched him sweat. Christopher sat nearby, tickling his fingers on the fake leather seats. He had the money. Her money in his wallet. He had said it was better this way. Everything kept together like a real marriage. A bargain between them. The shoe salesman rubbed his forehead. He held up his hands to say, 'No good.'

Christopher stood up. 'That's it then.'

Greta looked at the shoe shelves. There were so many.

'A different strap,' she told the salesman and he was on his feet to find something to fit the customer's curiously high instep. He had not seen such a footstep, he said in his precise English. He ran his fingers over the leather and straw shoes. She watched him milk romance out of the gesture. He had black hair and a crisp shirt but his sweat had made his face wet. He was anxious to choose the correct sandal for her foot. He was anxious to sell. Greta smiled at him.

Christopher said, 'Let's go.'

She said no to begin with. She concentrated on keeping her stomach tight and imagined that her feet were anchored inside the shop floor. He would not and could not move her. He lifted her up instead. The shoe man turned and watched them go. Greta turned and said goodbye as her husband steered her out onto the street.

The sun blasted down and the smell of urine followed them.

Young men in pressed trousers with their hate hidden behind zips and buttons. She saw a few turn faces towards certain walls and then urinate. Children played with dolls and cars. Nuns sidestepped and Christopher said nothing until they arrived back at the pensione. He said she would have to make do with the shoes she had.

'I'm not made of money.'

*

That was what marriage was. A bargain and an adventure for life.

'My money too,' she reminded him. She sat on the edge of the bed. 'My money too,' she insisted.

He didn't hit her and she thought perhaps everything would be fine. He whistled as he fixed his tie.

All for dinner this evening with the other honeymooning couple.

If the other wife took out a cigarette, the other husband rushed to light it. If she needed wine, he ordered it. If she turned her face, he snatched at her lips with his mouth.

The other husband, Greta thought.

Another husband, she wondered.

Her husband had been so lovely once and now as he walked about their room, Greta heard the silence climb out from the walls and her armpits grew wet and her stomach slicked. Something. She had to find something to say to him.

'Something,' she whispered.

'What?' he said. His eyes were black and shining in his head. 'What something?'

'Nothing,' she said.

She never told him that she had nearly drowned off the Isle of Capri.

Tumbleweed

Emma McKervey

Somehow it has become a ritual, or at least a symbol,
that shot panned wide over the empty expanse,
and the tumbleweed skimming through the neglected space.
It bounces like a bomb towards a dam because it means
something imminent; the pause, the calm before the holy stranger.
The tumbleweed is a twisted wreath looking for a head.
In a reality that is not a movie tumbleweeds exist to root them-
selves,
the hard tangle bearing seeds for safe dispersal far across the
Eurasian steppe,
moving westwards, hiding in boxes of grain to leapfrog the seas,
then continuing the vagabond roll stateless from state to state.
This rootless plant; deadened and detached by circumstance,
seeking
clear earth for its young, casting its thirsty self throughout the
dry lands.
They catch sometimes in fences, against high walls, building up
so that they need cutting out; and at crossroads, trapped at the
point
of many turns, so it becomes impossible to know just how to go
on.

Birdgirl

Geraldine Mills

Light, like water, finds its own way, spills into brightness through the gaps in the curtains. It reaches Leila's eyelids. They open. The girls in the other bunks are already up and gone. Except Masha, in the bed above, who has finally fallen into an unsettled sleep after everything. She cries out a name Leila does not recognise. 'Hush,' she whispers, 'you're OK. Everything is OK.'

The door shucks open and the man stands there, his face bleak with anger when he sees she's not dressed. 'Didn't I tell you to be ready,' he says, tapping the face of his wristwatch with his stained fingernail.

Leila secretes herself into her clothes. The cold of the floor scalds the soles of her feet. 'I hope you'll be alright,' she hears a waking Masha whisper as she creeps out the door.

In the other room the man has brewed coffee, is eating the last slice of bread. Small rivers of condensation run down the windowpanes by the sink. He pours the black liquid into two mugs. There's nothing else to eat but a green pepper. Leila bites into it as if it's a bright sweet apple.

'Time to go,' the man says. 'Remember what I told you?'

Leila ties up her boots and slips her hands through her bubble-coat sleeves. The man walks ahead of her to the bus stop, all the time talking into his phone in a voice that will not tell her whether it's good or bad. Probably another truck sneaking in, packed like seeds in a poppy pod. Body smells. No one making a sound. Sharing the one breath.

Like when she came.

The bus takes the road running along by the sea to the centre of the town. She presses her nose to the glass, looking at women in designer shoes walking their ratty little dogs along the path as waves push themselves onto the strand. Others jogging, weaving in and out through the strollers. Masha said there are people here whose houses have rooms just for their outdoor gear or pets' bowls. Even the dogs bark differently in this place. She looks out at the islands that rise from the water like newly discovered monsters coming up for air.

The man said her parents would follow very soon, but it's months now. No word from them.

'Hurry, hurry,' he says, as they get off the bus. 'You'd better not lose the best spot, if you know what's good for you.'

Shoppers walk by with their umbrellas up, thinking that the only thing that falls from the sky is rain, but Leila knows. She knows right down to the scars on her legs. She misses her mother's voice, her father's, the way they played their own music together. The walls of their house drinking it in, her ears drinking it. Hoping that one day …

… but she mustn't think of that, now.

The man hurries them up Small Street, past the tap dancer rising sparks from the cobblestones, along Big Street where a teenager carries a loaf of bread on his arm as if he's going to play a tune on it; down Wide Street where shopkeepers are putting out their stands onto the open pavement and call Saturday greetings to one another. She will not learn the true names of the streets in this town. She promises herself that. Not until she can learn them with her mother, her father.

The man stops at a clearing on the pavement near the market, where most people have to pass by to get to where they want to go.

'This is the place,' he says as he drops the tin box on the ground in front of her. Leila is all shaky inside.

'You can't stand there, it's my pitch,' a woman with long beaded hair and a basket of threads shouts at them, but the sculptor, crouched beside her making a sand statue, hits back, 'Leave the young girl alone, she can stand anywhere she fuckin' likes.'

He returns to shaping the ears of his sand horse. Leila doesn't believe he carved it all himself. He'd have had to have been there before cockcrow to get it to that shape. It's too complete. He's pretending too, but because of his kindness, she says, 'Thank you, your sand horse is beautiful.'

He winks back at her and smooths the already clean lines on the back of the sculpture.

Leila's belly is doing somersaults when she thinks of all the practising she has done, for days and nights, the man standing over her, waving her passport at her, screeching when she got it wrong. Now he leans in towards her. 'What have you to remember?' he asks.

'Pretend I have feathers,' she answers.

She sticks her hands into her pockets, plants her feet firmly on the ground to steady herself. Starts. She has been using her fingers as a way to remember the order of them, so with her pointing finger by her side, she begins with the *tslepp tslepp tchurp* of the sparrow, chirruping like the little brown bird, as people scurry by, their collars pulled up against the damp day. They hear the sound and turn their heads, looking all around to see where it's coming from.

'That's not half bad,' a roly-poly woman says and walks on by, casting a glance at the empty tin.

The man stands on the other side of the street, his phone still to his ear, one eye watching her. No one is putting any money into the box, so he marches across and throws in a few cents. They fall, with their tinny song burst, against the metal. Leila twitters again. A woman with an overloaded shopping bag, vegetables and flowers sticking out of it, grapples with her purse and drops in a coin. Leila smiles and sings back her thanks.

Then a woman pushing a buggy, with a little boy in it, pulls up in front of her. The child claps his joy-filled hands, and she sings, making him chuckle. The woman undoes his restraints, gives him a coin and lets him toddle over.

He leans down and waits for the euro to fall into the tin. As she completes another little chirp, he puts his chubby hand down again to take his money back. 'No, Jack,' the mother says, 'it's for that poor girl,' and pulls him out of the box, screaming. Whisks him away into the morning shoppers.

So, this is what she has become.

The woman's words send her shame mounting. Drives her mind blank. What was the next song on her list? Then she remembers what she must remember, her little game, naming her fingers for each bird sound so she can recall them: middle finger: skylark. How her parents polished their instruments before they handed them over. The money they got for them. Her passage paid. They may as well have pulled their arms from their sockets, leaving them limbless.

It was the first thing she ached for when she came. Music. Found it the other side of the window of that awful room where they now lived. She listened, gathering into the core of her the sounds they all made, learning, learning, identifying the difference between the throat song of each one.

The day the man heard her.

As she calls out the song of the skylark, followed by the *switt switt switt* of the swallow, two girls about her age, in navy tracksuits, walk by, scrolling on their phones, sharing some new text, new Instagram. They see her. Snigger. 'Look at your one tweeting,' the taller of them says. 'And she doesn't even have a phone,' the shorter girl smirks back, aiming her camera at her. It will be up on TikTok before the morning is over. Leila is sure of that.

The only way she can steady herself, get back at them, is to copy the peacock. When she reproduces the skirling high notes, a little girl in a fluffy pink coat puts her hands to her ears. 'Like screeching bagpipes,' she says, but before she runs away, Leila is back on track again and softens her shame with the *koo koo koo*

135

kuru of the wood pigeon. The little girl puts her thumb in her mouth and waits to hear the linnet's sweet notes, followed by the *choy choy choy churee* of thrush, singing its own song twice.

That one gets people to gather around. A man in a flat cap and baggy trousers asks, 'Can you make the sound of a hen and her chicks?'

It's not on her finger list but it's easy because she remembers Grandmother's farmyard, the hens scratching the dirt, searching out the shadow places where they laid their warm brown eggs. How she gathered their gifts, let them nestle in her open hands.

First, she cheeps the tiny cheeping sounds of the chick. Then a clucking hen. The woman with the blue hair says, 'It's just like the sound the hen makes when it's laying. *Keark keark keark.*'

Everyone laughs.

Claps.

She thinks of the nuggets and chips she's been promised, if she makes enough money. She sings some more.

She can't help smiling when she calls out the owl sound, because it gives her heart, thinking of the little night bird that was on the covers of her bed at home, wherever it is now. It feels like she's talking to him when she repeats her short hoot, a pause and then the rapid hooing. *Too-wit too-hoo.*

As she finishes, the woman with the blue hair asks: 'Hey, loveen, are you on your own?'

Leila looks across to where the man stands, still talking, still watching her. He puts his hand to his other ear.

'Oh, no,' she reassures the interrogator. 'There's my uncle, he's just gone to get me a drink of juice,' and points him out as she was told to do.

After the woman has moved away to study the ankle boots in one of the shop windows the man hurries across. 'What did she want?'

She repeats what she has said. 'Well, back to work,' he says glancing down to see what's in the box. 'Keep them coming.'

There are lots of requests for more skylarks, for great tits and robins. She knows them well, they're on her finger list too. She calls and whistles, scolding sounds, wistful sounds, the rolling churr of the wren, bird sounds that come from her throat and into the street as people stand in front of her with hot buttery croissants wrapped in greasy paper. They take big bites of them, wipe the crumbs from their mouths and throw any leftover change into the box. The scent of the pastries, the hollow nourishment of the green pepper, the promise of warm food afterwards keeps her going.

Inside, she has held her best one until last. She starts on the first note. It comes out clear and sweet. It gives her courage, so she tries the next and the next, building up note by note to the very sweetest until the street is full of sunny mornings and trills. People stop, not believing where the sound is coming from.

'Do you hear that?' they say.

'So close to the real thing, it makes no difference.'

'So pure, so true.'

She whistles again, keeping the notes going, as if she had feathers, like the man said. More and more coins thrum as they drop into the box before the passers-by step away with a smile on each face. She thinks of her mother, her father.

Then, from a treetop near the church, the sound is echoed back to her as clear as joy bells. The blackbird.

She sings.

Its full voice rejoices in return.

She repeats his phrasing.

Soon the whole street has come to a halt to hear girl and bird call back and forth to one another. Before long silent notes mingle with coins in the box. The look on the man's face.

Call Back

Eleanor Hooker

See you in two years, the nurse had said,
a shock then, a week later to receive
a call back – all certainty fell away
beneath my feet, as though,
overtaken by my own life, I'd been
sailing unwary and about to capsize.

In the clinical rooms, silence
is flawless, and worry a creature we pet.
Stripped to the waist and vulnerable,
we wear pink cotton capes back to front.

The technician who presses my breast
between X-ray plates has forgotten,
if ever she knew, that each woman in her pink
cotton cape is the central character in her own
story, and she is neither kind nor gentle.

The doctor tells me, from my previous scan
there's evidence of change – nothing sinister,
and, seeing me flounder, is considerate.
She lays her hand on my arm, steadies my boat,
tells me she's confident it's 'all clear'.

I think of my friend, who, years ago, was called
back for a pass/fail viva, who sobbed
over and over that she'd *nearly failed* and I,
confounded, asked of her, would you
prefer to be nearly drowned, or nearly saved?

When I emerge Peter is waiting, pacing.
I feel the ground rise up to steady me,
and finally I get why my friend was so distraught
all those years ago. I am given leave to return
to my life, aware it could have been otherwise.

Ablaze
(an extract from
Bright Burning Things)

Lisa Harding

There she is, lethal and irresistible, my high-kicking sidekick, and there goes that minx of a song, 'Impossibly Beautiful', and there is the sky so high and the light so bright and the sand warm velvet beneath the soles of my bare feet, and here comes the rush, an intense feeling of connection with all that is right and good in this world: my son's sticky hand in mine as he stares at the sky, my dog trotting alongside, his black coat glinting in the sunlight.

'Don't look directly at the sun, sweetheart, it burns your eyes.'

'But Yaya, you do it too.'

I bend to kiss him on the forehead, over and over as he laughs and pretend-wrestles me away. We look like everyone else as we skip down Sandymount Strand, dogs and kids, a mark of normality. No man, but then that's not unusual these days. Tommy breaks free and he careens like a drunk – no, that won't do, push that one away – runs unsteadily towards the surf, the frothy tongues of water that lick the sand. 'Go, Herbie, go – mind Tommy!' The dog bounds after him and the two of them frolic at the water's edge and I feel wave after wave of delicious things, my body vibrating with them, fingertips electric, heat pulsing its way through me.

The fever builds and I find I'm stepping out of my trousers and pulling my T-shirt over my head, dropping them in a puddle at my feet before I sprint towards my boys. My imp is waving, beckoning me into the shimmering water. *Hello, Elation, you spangly bitch.* I'm in my bra and knickers, but that's OK because it's hot and others are in their swimsuits and my underwear could pass for a bikini, so this is fine this is fine this is fine. Herbie is barking wildly. He'd have been put down in a week's time, they said, if I hadn't taken him then. Who rescued who? – the thought rises as I am submerged, the cold a tingle, adding to all the other tingles of the day, and my head is under and it's silky salty down here.

My body feels strong as I push through the surge of water, the sunlight refracted like so many tiny stars, until my lungs are burning, and my heart is thrumming in my throat. I turn on my back and float, staring directly at the concentration of light. When I close my eyes a carnival of colours and shapes explodes behind my lids. Oh, Mr Sunshine's working his magic all right! I crane my neck to see my boys, but there's a stranger, bending down to talk to Tommy. A distorted version of the happy song of moments before burrows and grooves. Now the stranger is picking him up. Not OK. Strike at the sea with sharp, staccato strokes, fluid sloshing in my ears and mouth. As soon as my feet hit the shallows I sprint, pushing the body of water away as if it were mere air.

'It's OK, it's OK, sweetheart, I'm here now, I'm here,' I say, or I think I say, my voice warped and bouncing in my ears as I open my arms to gather him up.

'You really shouldn't leave a little one alone like that,' the stranger says, an old woman who's cradling Tommy too close. 'Here,' and she reaches into her bag to hand me a towel. 'Where are your clothes?'

I don't like the aura of authority about this woman who still hasn't let go of my son. Start to shake with anger and cold, purple patches breaking out on my arms and legs.

'It's OK, Herbie,' I say as I pat the dog on the head.

'Oh, that poor creature belongs to you? I thought it was a stray.'

The woman's voice sounds like a swarm of something biting and black, with wings. Static builds up inside my head, so I have to shake it.

'Are you OK, dear?' falls out of the woman's mouth, and it stings.

'Jesus, I'm fine, OK? Perfectly fucking fine. Now just give me back my boy and we'll be out of your way.'

The woman's grip on Tommy tightens. 'Perhaps you should dry yourself off first?'

Shaking with something else now and it's rocking me deep inside. My voice is huge and swallowed and I'm scared of what might happen if I release it. Breathe: in, out, in, out.

The woman sucks in her cheeks, biting down on them, making her appear cadaverous, as if she might spirit Tommy away to another dimension. 'Is there someone I can call?' Her voice a hag's voice. I knock the phone out of her hand and grab my son from her arms, which are stick-thin with loose swathes of skin. Feel repulsed by this old woman: her proximity, her bossy intrusion into our happy, happy world.

The woman calmly bends to pick up her phone, which makes my reaction seem all the more extreme. Even when I can see myself like this, from the outside, I still can't stop the tornado whipping up through me: a 'child thief', a 'kiddy fiddler', a 'dirty old bag', 'witch/bitch/crone/cunt' rip out of me as I run, a bawling Tommy clasped tight to my sopping bra, Herbie in step. Sprint to the car without stopping to pick my clothes up off the sand, people are staring – let them stare, they have nothing better to do. I throw Tommy in the back with Herbie – whose hair on his back is standing up, hyena-like – before I turn the key, which I left on the front right-hand tyre (a trick Howard taught me as I was forever losing my keys – good for something, the prick). Rev the engine and move away from the packed car park on to the congested road, my bare feet slipping on the pedals.

I put the heater on full, willing my old banger on, humming one of Tommy's favourite tunes: *Mary had a little lamb, little lamb, little lamb* ... Usually when I hum he sings, his cartoon-angel-like voice high and pure, but this time he just sticks his thumb in his mouth and sucks on it hard, as if worrying it might make the other thoughts go away. 'OK, little man?' I say in the rear-view mirror and smile, giving him the thumbs up. Nothing. Try again: 'OK, big man?' I stick my tongue out, roll it so the two sides touch off each other, which would normally make him chuckle, then roar with laughter, but he just squeezes his eyes shut and sucks more intently. 'OK, Mister Man, we'll be home soon, and we can have some fishy fingers and jumping beans, OK?' I turn on the radio and Ravel's *Bolero* blasts from the speakers.

As the car heats, fog forms on the windows. I draw a heart on the windscreen, keeping one hand on the steering wheel, and write *Mummy loves you* inside it. 'Tommy, look.' I trace the letters with my fingertip, reading aloud. He opens his eyes, squinting, leans into Herbie, tries to hug him, arms only reaching a third of the way around his wide girth. The dog moans, a happy contented sound. 'Good boy, Herbie, best boy.' His thick tail thumps on the tatty nylon seats. 'My best boys, what would I do without you?' At the next traffic light, a man beside us nods madly, winds his window down and shouts: 'It's not every day. Lucky day. Lucky me. Alright, darlin'?' I ignore him until the traffic lights shift to green, when I give him the finger as I speed off, tendrils of his voice hanging in the air: 'Yup, I'd like that alright ...' My adrenalin spikes as I realise he's following me, or is he, or is that mad imp deluding me? 'Not too long now,' I say to my two boys in the back, who are still cuddled into each other. I turn to the right, checking the mirror, and see him still, but then, no, it's not him, he was just having his fun, harmless fun, it's OK it's OK it's OK. My heartbeat slows down as I think of the promise waiting for me in the fridge. I'm glad I had the foresight to do that: chill it. It's hot in the car now and it's still warm outside.

Pulling up at the row of tiny terraced red-bricked cottages, I pray that none of the snoops are lurking behind their half-slatted blinds. That Mrs O'Malley always butting in, dropping in home-made bread for 'the little mite'. I know how to make Tommy happy with his orange food: his cornflakes and marmalade and beans and fish fingers and Cheddar cheese. Meat is dead animal flesh, I had to tell him that. Not the fish, though, I don't tell him about the fish being hooked and whacked over the head. He won't eat anything remotely resembling green – something to do with mould. He's not undersized or anything, but then I don't know any other four-year-olds. I cover myself as best I can with the skimpy towel and run up the tangled path to the front door, painted a shocking pink by my own hand, sploshed and botched. 'Let yourselves in,' I shout as I tear into the one bedroom we all share. I rip off my wet underwear and open the top drawer, a jumble of socks, bras and knickers, manage to locate a clean pair, before finding myself in the kitchen in just my pants in front of the fridge.

'Yaya, you've no clothes on.' Tommy's voice is at the kitchen door. I hear his footsteps padding into the front room, the tip-tapping of Herbie accompanying him, then the sudden burst of noise as the TV blares. 'Too loud,' I shout. He doesn't lower the volume – maybe he didn't hear me, or maybe he's trying to annoy me. I twist the top off the bottle and am tempted to glug from the neck, need to cool, to soothe, but force myself to open a cupboard and get a glass. A mark of staying civilised, even with no one to witness me. Particularly with no one to witness me. This delicate white deserves a glass, the space to aerate. Pour, sip daintily, then throw my neck back and drink the whole thing in one go. Instantly I relax. How tense that woman made me feel, that man in the car – *other people, fuck them* – and I pour myself a second glass. A faint burning in my stomach, a mellow warmth spreading in my chest. By the third I find I can swallow, breathe, swallow, breathe. Like swimming.

I turn the grill on to 180 degrees, open the freezer to take out the fish fingers, and find there are none. I rummage through the cupboards, locate two cans of baked beans and one opened can of dog food, a bit rank, but should be OK, Herbie eats anything. Stick the beans in the microwave and slip my frilly apron over my pants, an ironic moving-in gift from Tina, back when we shared a flat in London: 'To my favourite domestic goddess!' I see my old pal, grinning, off her face pretty much all the time on anything at all. The beans are hissing and spitting, jumping out of their skins. The microwave is spattered with bean juice. Later. I'll clean that later.

'Anything good on?' I place the dog's plate on the couch beside him and Tommy's plate on his knees.

'Where are the fishies?'

'Don't start, Tommy. Remember the starving children in Africa?' The moment I say it I wish I could force the words back inside. The kind of shit my father used to spew at me. 'There was none left. We'll get some tomorrow, OK?'

Tommy nods and lifts a spoon to his mouth. 'Ouchy.'

'Too hot, darling?' I go to his plate and blow. 'There now, see … yummy?' Lift the spoon and make an airplane noise as I bring it towards his mouth, which is clamped shut. See my hand moving of its own accord, slamming the spoon against his lips and forcing them to open. The clang of metal as the spoon falls from my shaking hand onto the floor. Hyper imaginings, never a good sign. 'OK, not to worry, you'll eat when you're hungry.' I manage a jaunty wink before finding myself back in the kitchen, the bottle to my mouth, to hell with decorum, *be still my banging heart.*

The bottle emptied, a space opens up and my head feels liberated, as if I've just removed a too-tight elasticated band from my hair. Glide into the living room and flop down between my two boys, Tommy feeding Herbie the rest of his beans by hand: what a sweet, caring boy. I'll make sure he eats later. Settle against the warmth of their bodies, feel mine softening, falling.

*

Sometime later an acrid smell of burnt cheese on toast from yesterday fills the room. I sit up too fast, head banging, dots dancing in my eyes. Black smoke is billowing under the kitchen door. Move as if in a trance, groggy, but pulse racing – is this another of my night hallucinations? Open the grill door, reach in, grab the handle, flames are leaping, drop the pan onto the floor, *fuck, be still my walloping head.* Wrap my hand in a soggy tea towel and lift the pan into the sink. Under the tap, and whoosh, the flames burst and die, black charcoal in their place. I lined the grill with baking paper instead of tinfoil, stupid stupid stupid woman. I see my son in the doorway, eyes huge and glassy. 'OK, Tommy, everything's alright now.'

He smiles, his mouth tight and tilted, an exact replica of his grandfather, and says, 'Beeootiful. Hot and slinky like the sun.'

Herbie whines. My hand is hot and scalded.

'Water, Yaya.' I smile at him, my little oracle, and hold my hand under the cold tap.

Every window will need to be opened. Every part of me is jangling. Feel myself crashing, falling into the pit. Should've known when I first saw her there on the beach, shimmering, irresistible, that this was the way it would go. Grab the full bottle, turn my back, undo the screw top with my teeth. Tell myself that what Tommy doesn't see can't hurt him.

♥

Rock Musical for The Diceman (an extract)

Ferdia Mac Anna

DRAMATIS PERSONAE

THE DICEMAN, narrator, Greek chorus and performance artist in search of immortality.

FRANKIE BOONE, 21-year-old badge-seller and chancer who dreams of rock stardom.

REB, Frankie's employee and punk wannabe.

DEBS, college dropout, wants to find a new life that doesn't involve getting her heart broken or having to study Chaucer. She's a bit mysterious.

SHIV, Frankie's ex, wants to take over the world one hair salon at a time. Also wants Frankie back – maybe.

MELISSA (MEL), Shiv's boss, almost psychotically eager to please and who allows few thoughts in her head to remain unspoken.

SCENE 1

A tall figure in a cape appears, walks slowly to the front of the stage. THE DICEMAN, our narrator and street performance artist. FRANKIE, SHIV, REB and MEL form a line behind him, their backs to us. THE DICEMAN strikes a pose and freezes. We hear muted chords on an electric guitar as DEBS walks to the stage from the audience. THE DICEMAN holds the pose as DEBS goes to him, takes a close look. She walks away, but something makes her stop. Is he looking at her? She turns to look. Instantly, THE DICEMAN gives her an outrageous wink. DEBS smiles, and she walks away to take her place in line as THE DICEMAN slowly walks to the front of the stage and sings 'Diceman Shoes'.

THE DICEMAN (sings).
    As I was walking out on Grafton Street
    I met everyone
    That I would ever need
    As I was walking out on Grafton Street
    I met everyone
    That I would ever need

    I'm the living breathing winking news
    No one fills
    My Diceman shoes.

The song ceases. THE DICEMAN draws closer to the audience, singling out individual sections of the audience to address, leer at, wink at, smile or otherwise engage.

THE DICEMAN.
    Ladies and gentlemen, skins and punks
    In the summer of '77, our economy is sunk
    Tribes are gathered in the Dandelion Green
    The open-air market is where we set out our scene
    Permit me to introduce myself
    I am The Diceman, street performance artist and fully-grown elf.

    I came among you as an April Fool
    Flung out of Glasgow by the handiest route
    Reborn in Dublin as the Dandelion Clown
    A mute mannequin – am I real or just kidding around?
    My visual displays enrich, outrage, amuse by fripperies

Shoppers, tourists, passers-by, skins, mods, boot boys, even hippies.

People question my motives, surely it's plain to see
My art is myself – a quest for immortality?
For what use is living if bound by rules applicable
Welcome everyone to the incandescent and inexplicable.

Aromas of Indian oil. Veggie burgers from the Hare Krishnas
Sweet pang of urine from the jacks or a restaurant kitchen
Where dive-bombing seagulls meet clippety-clopping pedestrians
There you'll find me, still as a lighthouse
Astride an invisible horse
An immobile equestrian.

The cast gather around him.

Tapestries of hair, eyes, noses and lips
pause at my feet to wonder –
Is it I a man?
Marilyn Monroe?
Mother Nature's blunder?

If the kids are good, drop money in my cap
I give them a wink, blow a kiss or chase them
– just like that.

He chases the cast and they scatter, and then regroup behind him

THE DICEMAN.
   Until the Gardaí told me
   I constituted an obstruction
   A threat against society.
   They threatened legal abduction.

Mr Diceman, you're a bad influence.
To an impressionable population
Grafton Street packed with human statues
Performance artists, buskers, magicians – a humiliation of the
nation.

But there's no law against strolling
Millimetres at a time
Inching forward in slow-mo
Is never a crime.

Now I'm a walking installation
They can't touch me, my friends.
Dressing room is Freebird Records
My performances never end.

*

SCENE 4

DEBS is being interviewed by SHIV and MEL for a job on the clothing stall. The others look on.

SHIV. What makes you think I need another assistant?
DEBS. Well, I need a job and I like clothes.
SHIV. Do I look like I need help?
DEBS. You put up a sign saying 'Assistant Wanted'.
MEL. You seem like a nice person. Are you?
DEBS. Am I nice?
MEL. Yes.
DEBS. I have my moments.
SHIV. Are you sussed? Or do you just do your own thing?
DEBS. Pardon?
MEL. She means can you handle the public?
DEBS. Oh. Well, I worked in my uncle's bar last summer.

MEL. See, she's sussed.

SHIV. Those two lads in the badges stall are looking at you. Do you know them?

DEBS looks at FRANKIE and REB, who wave at her.

DEBS. Maybe I know them from somewhere

MEL. Frankie there – see the dark-haired one?

DEBS. I see him.

MEL. Well guess what? (*long beat*). He used to go out with Shiv.

SHIV. One date. That's not going out. That's an audition. And he failed.

MEL. He didn't call her. She had to phone him.

SHIV. OK, another test. This country's totally fucked.

DEBS. Is that a question?

SHIV. Would you agree?

DEBS. What's that got to do with the job?

SHIV. Well, there's four million in the country. Right?

DEBS. Kind of.

SHIV. That's a million on the dole. A million emigrating, a million in school, and everyone else works for Fianna Fail.

MEL. Don't mind her. No way there's a million people in Fianna Fail.

SHIV. So why should I give you a job where there's so many others who deserve a chance. What makes you different?

DEBS. Keep your job then.

MEL. That's a joke. Don't mind her – she's only trying to see how you cope under pressure. Excuse us a moment, will you?

DEBS. OK.

SHIV takes MEL to one side.

SHIV. I don't like her.

MEL. She seems OK. And we need an extra pair of hands.

SHIV. She's a bitch.

MEL. That's what you said about me. Now look at us.

SHIV. Well, you're my boss. I can call you whatever I like.

MEL. Let's give the girl a break. Try her out for a day. If it doesn't work, fine.

SHIV. Looks like a bitch to me.

MEL. You have a very peculiar outlook sometimes.

SHIV. Can you blame me? The state of things.

MEL and SHIV return to where DEBS has been watching.

MEL. She won't be happy till she's in charge of everything. She tried for president of the students' union in UCD. It didn't work out. She's still banging on about it. Anyway, congrats, you've got the job. Can you start right away?

DEBS. I don't know if I want it now.

MEL. Course you do.

MEL leads DEBS away while SHIV glowers.

MEL. And there's a big ceili tonight and everyone's going. We'll have great craic.

THE DICEMAN.

The Diceman's prom is about to commence.

Choose your partners, it's going to be immense.

Ceili music begins. The boys line up stage right; the girls stage left. Each group holds hands as they dance the 'Aon dó trí. Suddenly, the music changes to a fast punky tune. Everyone pogo-dances. Everyone goes wild. Suddenly THE DICEMAN stumbles towards the back of the stage as the music changes to discordant alarm. THE DICEMAN mimes physical distress and lurches theatrically before the others catch and hold him. Slowly, THE DICEMAN straightens himself. He clicks his fingers in a slow rhythm as he regains his composure. On the fourth click he signals the music to begin and the music changes to a bluesy rock tune. FRANKIE puts his hand on one of THE DICEMAN's shoulders, DEBS puts hers on the other. THE DICEMAN slowly walks forward. As he begins to sing, the cast spreads out either side, clicking their fingers in time and joining in the chorus.

THE DICEMAN.

One day I'm walking round like Marilyn

The next time you see me, I'm wearing angel wings

One day I'm walking round like Marilyn

The next time you see me

I'm wearing angel wings
I'm the living, breathing, walking news
No one fills my Diceman shoes.

CAST (*sing softly*). Diceman shoes.

Repeat as music grows softer. THE DICEMAN nods at each player in turn to dismiss them. As each character leaves, he or she ceases finger-clicking. FRANKIE and DEBS are the last to go. Only THE DICEMAN remains, clicking his fingers in time to the music, striking various poses.

THE DICEMAN.

No one fills my Diceman shoes. (*THE DICEMAN gives a big wink.*)

Lights down. Music ceases.

END.

First Date

Ann Hickey

Peter and I had circled one another over the year and now finally he had asked me for an official date. Peter was handsome and had a great sense of humour. He suggested he take me to dinner and would we go to a film after that. I was beside myself with excitement – my first real date. However, I summoned up all my courage and asked if instead of the pictures, we could go to the Gate Theatre – Oscar Wilde's *Lady Windermere's Fan* was playing there. And Peter, being the gentleman he was, said it was no problem.

We met at 6 p.m. under Clerys Clock on O'Connell Street, as so many star-struck lovers had met before us. Imagine my excitement when Peter announced he was taking me to the Paradiso Restaurant in Westmoreland Street. There was no slumming it in McDonald's for us. The entrance to the Paradiso was up a very narrow, twisting staircase, the walls of which were adorned with photographs of the rich and the famous, film stars and politicians, who had all graced the Paradiso with their presence at some time or other.

We were greeted by the maître d' who escorted us to our table and held out my chair for me with an exaggerated flourish and placed the linen napkin on my lap. Peter had worked in Jammet's restaurant and was well versed in fine dining, but it was all new for me. I had scampi for the first time and loved it. No wine or alcoholic drinks as none of my circle of friends drank or indeed smoked. However, despite such heroic self-sacrifice, I went on to sin big time by having Pavlova for dessert.

Afterwards, we strolled back up O'Connell Street holding hands (very risqué) past the Metropole – 'the ballroom of romance' – then on to the GPO, which played such an important role in our struggle for a free Ireland, and of course the wonderful Nelson's pillar. I, to my shame – like so many Dubliners – never paid my sixpence to climb the spiral staircase to the top to see the beautiful 360-degree panoramic views of Dublin.

Looking down O'Connell Street, I saw the Rotunda Assembly Rooms. This was the first maternity hospital to be built in the British Empire. A Dr Bartholomew Mosse built it, investing his own private money as well as fundraising widely. It was to be a hospital for the poor women of Dublin, who were giving birth in the most appalling and unsanitary conditions. He laid out pleasure gardens for the world of fashion, complete with walks, amphitheatre, orchestra, temples for refreshment and assembly rooms for balls, routs and concerts. The whole complex was built in the eighteenth century and the aristocracy of the day would come and be entertained to a classical concert in the Rotunda (aptly named when you think of the shape of things to come) after which they would retire to what is now the Gate Theatre for supper and to play cards. Beneath the Gate was the most magnificent ballroom where the gentry would dance the night away. Poor Dr Mosse exhausted himself from work and financial worry and died an early death at forty-six years of age.

I loved the Gate Theatre with its Georgian decor. The ambiance was wonderful. It was truly a real night out. Through the years my father had taken us there. The two back rows sold for a shilling: they were chipped wooden seats and were most uncomfortable. At some stage Lord Longford increased the cost of the seats to one shilling and sixpence. My father was outraged and swore he would never darken the door again, he would boycott the Gate.

This of course never happened and he paid the exorbitant price, but grumbled.

As Peter and I were swept up the beautiful staircase of the theatre, I was, as always, conscious of all the wonderful people in history in whose footsteps I was following. This was further reinforced when I saw, as always, Lord Longford standing at the top of the steps to the left, warmly welcoming us all. As we stood in the foyer, dramatic melodic music floated out, classical, of course, no bang-a-bang stuff here. The stage extended out beyond the curtain drop and perched on the left was a baby grand piano at which a man, resplendent in black tails, would proceed to play the most exciting classical music.

Lord and Lady Longford (Edward and Christine Pakenham) had come to the aid of the ailing Gate, all from their own private funds, when it ran into financial trouble. I was fascinated: this was my first encounter with a real lord and lady. Lord Longford was a small rotund figure with a sweet, cherubic face, a wonderful smile and an engaging, warm personality. The two seats nearest the exit door were reserved each night for them both. There they sat, night after night. The Gate was really their baby as unfortunately they had no children of their own, and so the title passed to Lord Longford's younger brother Frank. Lord Longford, not surprisingly, was always fundraising. Each night you would find him in the foyer shaking his collection box vigorously under your nose and tripping you up on the way out, but always with a wonderful smile.

Lady Longford, on the other hand, was quite reserved and shy and not inclined to engage with the theatre-goers. She would slip quietly away backstage seconds before the interval and also seconds before the final curtain. Her hair was cut in the Parisian bob style and always looked very chic. Christine was somewhat stooped over at the shoulders, which only seemed to add to the wonderful persona, and she always had a clutch bag squeezed under her arm.

Peter had not been to the Gate before, but I was in my element, the play dealing with themes of honour, deceit and the futility of women's lives in olden times. At the interval we went for refreshments. The Gate had these tiny, tiny coffee cups. I loved them. The cups were so tiny you could only hold the handle with your thumb and forefinger and so your pinkie finger stood ramrod straight at an angle. Very affected. But this was the way I knew that real ladies drank their coffee. I would not normally drink coffee but when at the Gate I indulged with great delight. What a treat! And still to this day, it is a ritual with me. I simply must have a cup of coffee at the interval, even though, regretfully, the tiny cups have been consigned to history and the coffee will have me walking the floors during the night, unable to sleep.

Peter didn't enjoy the play that night. He thought the content was irrelevant and that we should live in the present, but he did find parts of it amusing. We chatted amiably as he escorted me to the bus stop and despite not loving the play, he asked me for another date, which I readily agreed to. When the bus finally arrived, a hasty peck on the cheek and off I went.

What a wonderful night. We were so young and oh so innocent.

Cadence
(in memoriam Andrew Kettle)
Eithne Lannon

It was not his absence
but what came after;

how silence begins
as a hollow,

a hesitation, a shift
in the gravity of meaning,

like a minor chord progression,
or a decrescendo that lingers.

There were movements in it,
subtle sounds insinuated,

the ambivalence of harmony
abbreviated,

how the bass clef
can become a closed listening,

an ear no longer ajar.
I can barely

hear the voice
of his fading frequency,

the slow tearing
into tonal extinction.

Even the light is too loud
for the symphony

of silence I now live in,
there's a gaping

matrix, a dark place
I slide into,

I have felt his ghost
soften

into the shape
of the space around me,

I hunker
at the edges of erasure –

now I know
how a man can die

before death
reaches

into him.

A Whisper of the Blizzard in the Hills Far Off

Niall McArdle

Are you mad? Out in this? You shouldn't be on the road at all. You're crawling along. You can barely see a thing, just a blurry grey and white howling around you as you shuffle around bends and turns and stamp on the clutch and wrestle with the gears, hoping the car won't stall.

You have the heat blasting. You turn up the radio to drown out the fan. The car is hobbling up a mountain against the wind and the sleet, and a song is screaming at you about, of all things, the *summer*.

Beside you, Ciara smiles. She's ten. She smiles a lot. You never know why. Her smile is a copy of her granddad's nasty smirk, lips rippling, like she's always enjoying a private joke.

Nobody can remember snow like this. The country's come to a halt. No buses. No trains. No bread. For some reason everyone thinks this is hilarious.

You think, Jenny won't be laughing. Grew up in the back of beyond in Canada, knows how treacherous it is to get behind the wheel in weather like this. *Spilled off the highway in the middle of nowhere. Twenty below. Stuck in a ditch three hours before a car came along, could've been three days.*

She knows real winter, knows properly cut off. *Can't even get a snow shovel in this ridiculous country.*

You know you won't get to the house in time. When you walk in, everyone will turn and look at you with salty eyes. They will leave you alone with your father only after you yell at them to get out.

The snow is heaving down now and thrumming against the windscreen. You switch the wipers to fast and listen to their steady, soothing whump-whump.

You know you'll be too late because you had a dream last night, of today's phone call and this blizzard and this drive up the mountain, and in the dream, you arrive twenty minutes after he dies.

You will drive on and up the mountain and when you reach a peak it will only be the half peak, miles of snow and drift and ice to crawl through, and this moment was also in the dream, and you will curse and slam the dashboard, and then you will try to remember if you cursed and slammed the dashboard in the dream.

The snow will be falling at the cemetery when they lower him into the ground, too. It will be soft and gentle, though, as though the universe was offering a kindly tribute to the dear departed.

The idea has you barking a guffaw, a sudden bursting 'Ha!' that somehow times itself with that exact same note of the song coming from the radio. The synchronicity of it sets you off again and you almost lose control of the wheel in a splutter of hacking, honking laughter.

*

You, at Ciara's age, lying on the floor under the desk while he worked, you with your crayons and cartoon monsters, him with his files. The tappety-tap-tap of his fingers on the desk. Blueish pipe smoke snaking up to the ceiling. Legs crossed, one foot jittering to the jazz on the stereo.

The coal and oil stink of his shoe polish hits you. You roll down, then up, the window to let in a quick blast of air. You change the station and catch the end of a weather bulletin. You wonder what eejit in Met Éireann came up with the colour-coding system for the weather alerts. Yellow snow? Talk about taking the piss.

That one time you spilt ink on his files. His eyes ballooned. There was a swift hush in the room and an odd quake in the air.

You will feel that air again when you stand over his corpse.

You will look at him, papery hands crossed on his chest, white hair brushed back, and you will bow your head and mumble something, and if anyone sees you doing that, they'll make the mistake of thinking that you're praying.

You hit a patch of ice and spin and end up in a ditch. This wasn't in the dream. The wheels are spinning. In the rear-view mirror there's a filthy fountain of slush. You reverse slowly, going down further so the tyres can get enough grip and then you floor it so you can clamber back onto the road. There is a shudder and a horrific grinding sound.

From beside you, you can feel a rippling smirk.

You used to sit where she is, because you're crawling up the hill to your father's deathbed in *his* car, a clunker so old there's nothing automatic about any of it. The clock actually looks like a clock and there's an ashtray under the radio. He taught you how to drive in it on this very road.

'Hands at ten and two, Eamon. Check your mirrors.'

The gearstick thunked when you put it into third and the car lurched.

'Don't grind the gears, son! This is a delicate machine. You'll never please a woman if you manhandle her like that.'

'I'm trying, Da.'

'You certainly are.'

His little hiccupy chuckle and that waggle of his eyebrows when your mother used to mix up Bach and Beethoven, or when she pronounced Yeats to rhyme with Keats. Sly, snide remarks about how her spectacular beauty almost made up for the lack of anything going on upstairs, but all in good fun, pet, c'mon love, take a joke.

The sleet is bulleting the car. The wipers are whump-whumping like crazy but you're afraid the gale could still whip them right off.

You know that soon you will have to deal with the detritus of his life. How every tiny ridiculous thing will matter, every piece of paper he ever signed, every tie he ever wore, every pair of shoes he ever polished. You will pack his stuff into boxes. Things to keep. Things to throw away. Things for the charity shop.

You've already done this once. You and Jenny did it with Ciara's things, her dolls, her toys, her clothes, crammed her life into a few boxes.

You see Ciara quite a bit these days. You always do around her anniversary. Coming up on eight years now. Those long nights in the hospital, her stubbly head and her eyes as big as saucers, tubes in her stick arms and up her nose, she stayed cheery while you and Jenny were falling to pieces, and you thought, *Why is she so fucking happy? Surely she knows her time's up, she must know, our child's not stupid.*

Those eyes are looking at you now. The head is no longer a cue ball. She has her usual throng of curls.

You wish she would speak when she visits you. You have so many questions. You want to ask her about where she's come from, to tell you something you're sure you couldn't come up with yourself. You need to believe that you haven't conjured her from a corner of your mind.

Because ... because ... well, because, you don't want to end up like him. 'Dotty' is the word everyone in the family agreed on years ago, when he started leaving the keys in the fridge and getting turned around on the drive home. Dad's a bit dotty. Looks at you bewildered when you visit. Sometimes thinks his wife is his mammy. Asks where his granddaughter is, sure it's been ages since you and Jenny brought her to see us.

Your mother cries and sighs a lot, of course, but you've noticed she's also a lot chirpier these days. That time you saw her rolling her eyes behind his back when he came downstairs in his togs and said he was going for a swim in the Pacific.

You wonder has Ciara visited Jenny as well? Does she choose to speak to her mother but not to you?

After the child died, there was a gap between you and Jenny. She spent days in bed, curtains closed, not eating, thundering at you because you seemed to be coping so well. *Useless prick, you weren't even there when Ciara finally slipped away.* You couldn't get to the hospital in time because you were shunting along the road during the big freeze.

Now it's happening again, you hauling your battered car through a whiteout to get to a deathbed, only to arrive there too late.

You tap your wedding ring on the wheel. After the divorce you took it off, but soon missed the heft of it.

You look at your daughter. You want to know what she's thinking but your heart buckles at the possibility that she hates watching over you, keeping you company, comforting you in a car clunking up a hill.

Will the old man show up soon as well? Is it only a matter of time until you see him tappety-tap-tapping in a corner or sitting beside you in the car, urging you to slow down and moaning about the music on the radio?

Will you see him in the supermarket aisle or on the DART or will he be a guard directing traffic or the bus driver or the man behind the counter at the newsagent's? You think you'll be able to bear it, finding him everywhere because you know it will kill him to discover how mundane the afterlife is.

He'll never shut up about it. 'This is dreadful, Eamon.'

There's something else, though, something you don't know yet. And you won't have a dream of it first to prepare you, how soon you will discover you miss him, miss his little chuckle and his waggling eyebrows and his shoe polish, and how the missing of him will undo you, how you will be again in this car pulled over at the side of the road, a heap of snot and tears, thumping the steering wheel.

The hills behind you finally, a thin line of smoke rising up ahead and the snow still falling, your wipers are whump-whumping and the radio is blaring and then the storm eases right up and you can see the lights of the house. You brake and crunch to a stop and turn off the engine. The silence from the radio is a shocking slap. You look at the upstairs window and you know they're huddled around the bed tending to his body, your mother gently combing his hair. Ciara's gone. You squint and tell yourself you can see her tiny footprints trailing up the lane to the house.

The snow has stopped. The wind has vanished. There's a gaunt quiet around you, and all you want to do is sit in this car at the top of this mountain and listen for a whisper of the blizzard in the hills far off.

A Child Again

Brendan O'Leary

Oh to be …
The child wrapped
around your legs
with the smells
of the kitchen
from your apron.

Oh to be …
on your lap
reading the comics
with the smell
of your working man's
clothes.

Oh to be …
Lying on summer's grass
waiting to be called
inside for dinner
but when I run in,
you are not there.

Shticky Hocks

Rachel Blayney

Every year we piled into the back of our parents' car, a Ford Corsair, EIO 443. I had a thing for memorising number plates. My parents, two siblings and a rescue poodle with a dicky heart would make the trip to visit friends in Tipperary. I dreaded the long trip as I got woefully sick every time. Dad would drive erratically, always looking for and trying to light the next cigarette, then drive along with his window half open, flicking the ash out. I sat behind him. Mum would give us Quells travel sick pills and I tried to distract us with games of I Spy and Spot the Colour, but it never worked. I was six, my sister was eight and my brother was too young to count.

The relief, on arrival, of seeing the wide avenue, sloping down towards the house, lined by ancient oak and beech trees. Each year we would check to see if they had all survived the storms of winter. The avenue ended in a roundabout just by the front door, then on to the yard or off through the forest to the lake. There was so much space and so many animals here that I was in heaven. The family would greet us at the door as the old Labrador would start barking on hearing the car, setting off the Jack Russell. The mum, Sally, would shriek in a shrill voice, a great welcome, 'How good to see you again and do come in!' The dad, Richard, was a large, soft, smiling man with a gentle voice under a major thatch of a moustache. He was partially deaf. I often wondered if that was due to Sally's shrieking or if she was facilitating him. He seemed to hear Mum perfectly.

They had three boys and a girl, although it always felt like it was a large family as they were forever away doing amazing things. Lucy, the youngest, was eight. We always came bearing gifts such as a large crate of oranges fresh from the Smithfield Market and a great lump of meat. They owned a vast farm, in my eyes, but money was tight. Still, traditions were always maintained. We would dress for dinner. Mum said it was also practical as a long tweed skirt and polo neck were just the thing for the dark cold hallways and one fire in the sitting room. The kitchen was where all the action was to be found: incubating kittens, lambs or chicks in the lower Aga oven with the door open. Smells of freshly baked bread and Sally's famous rock buns, which lived up to their name when one cracked a floor tile one day on impact. The kettle seemed to be perpetually on the boil. It was homely and so many adventures were hatched there.

On this visit we were introduced to their new little pony, Blackbird. Mum was cautious: she noticed some traits in the pony's character that made her uncomfortable but I just saw pure joy. Anyway, next day we three girls decided we wanted to go down to the local sweet shop, Shticky Hocks, but it was miles away and would take ages so our absence would be spotted. Some genius suggested we take the pony and if we went bareback, two could ride, one walk and then swap round. It was a foolproof plan.

Off we set, sneaking the pony past the kitchen window. We were chatting, giggling and singing the whole way so it seemed we got there very quickly. We arrived at Shticky Hocks. We tied the reins of the pony's bridle in true cowboy fashion to the lamp post just outside and all went in together.

It was a tiny dark shop with a tall counter. I had to tip my head right back to see anything because behind the counter were shelves of enormous jars bearing treasures. We all put our money on the counter to see what we could get with it. With her long, bony, clawed fingers, Mrs Hock counted the money and told us what combinations we could afford. Two of these and three of those. I loved her four-for-a-penny toffees in the square white wrappers. She took the jar from the shelf and put it on the counter, lowering her arm into the tall jar. A talon would extend to the bottom and pick at a toffee and prise it away from all the others. They were always stuck together, the same every year, possibly even still the same sweets. She repeated this process slowly. I was bewitched by the finger. Having bought all our delights, said good bye and thank you, she would always reply, 'Do come again.' It was the same every year.

We went out into the sunshine to find the pony ... gone! Just half a bridle left slumped at the bottom of the lamppost. We took too long – someone should have stayed with him. All too late now, we were in hot water. It was such a long walk home and it still didn't give us a good excuse. We did try! We arrived home, gooey toffee dripping out the corners of the saturated bags, tired and fully aware that there would be cross words and consequences doled out by the two mums. They thought there had been an accident. I didn't think of that, so they were very relieved. The pony had come racing through the yard, passed the kitchen window in a lather, wearing only the top half of his bridle. When their anxiety had eventually settled, we were in for the consequences. We were under observation, unable to do anything or go anywhere without adult supervision. Well, for this year anyway. They never remember. There is always next year.

In the Middle of the Woods

Phil Lynch

In the middle of the woods
raindrops hang in knuckles
from bare bony branches
before they buckle under the swell
and drop in twisted patterns
to sunder away in streams
searching for a river.

There is a silence to the rain
from our warm vantage
inside the wall-length window.
We are gathered to work with our words
willing them to swell and drop and flow,
twelve hands at work together,
apostles writing future gospels.

Every drop must do its job
to navigate hurdles seen and hidden,
some make it to the river,
some never get beyond the fall
but all are here and real and now,
as real as every breath we make
before we break for food
and chat about the this and that

of lives well lived in many ways,
filling in our family frames,
regaling with more familiar tales
of poetic and artistic paths passed
before the one that brought us
to this place, to sit around this table
and clink our glasses
in unspoken celebration of ourselves.

When talk turned to the sport of kings,
the last thing on our minds,
in the zest of our musings,
would have been to place a bet
on which of us would be
the first to fall.

Emma's Wedding

Katie Boylan

I met my best friend Emma in secondary school. I don't remember how we became friends but now, over twenty years later, I can't imagine not being friends with her. From day one we just clicked. We had similar interests, likes and dislikes. We lived near each other so catching up at the weekend was simple too, which meant we were inseparable.

After school I went to DIT to study communications, she went to NCI to do accounting. We still kept up a friendship and saw each other all the time. The first summer after college we went to Spain, the second summer we did a J1 in San Diego together, the third summer we worked in London, followed by a two-week sun holiday before college started back.

We were very compatible on holidays and soon we were saving up all our money to spend it on cheap flights to the sun. On our weeks away with friends, all we wanted to do was sunbathe, read books, chill out and drink a few glasses of *vino tinto* in the evening. We would stay on loungers later than any of the others, catching the last of the evening sun. It was the quietest time at the pool so we'd chat about anything and everything. Our conversations ranged from our careers, politics and current affairs to what boys we liked, people we didn't like, who we were dating, who we wanted to date. We'd talk about hopes for the future, plans we wanted to make, places we wanted to see, what we'd do when we got married and we both insisted that the other person would be their bridesmaid. Sometimes we'd be there so late chatting that one of the other girls would shout down to us to hurry up or we'd never make it down to the port for drinks.

After college I went to Australia. Emma followed me over to start her year abroad just as I went home to get a 'real job' so this meant we spent the next two years apart. It was awful! I felt like I was missing a limb. We rang and texted and kept in touch by email and it was wonderful when we were both home and in the same time zone again.

Soon people around us started to get married. We were always at the singles' table, wondering when it would be our turn. Then Emma met Dan in work. She said it was just a casual thing but then he was mentioned more and more and I knew it was serious. I met him and liked him instantly. They spent more and more time together but thankfully he didn't like the sun that much so myself and Emma still went on sun holidays together and continued our sun-lounger chats.

Soon they moved in together and one day in early December she rang me as I was driving home from work. We were chatting for a good five minutes before she told me

'I have news – we're engaged!'

I was over the moon. The real wedding planning had begun. All those ideas we'd spoken about on sun loungers were now being talked about for real. I'd finally watch my best friend getting married! We toasted her news in town in the Porter House after she tried on numerous wedding dresses. She asked me to be her chief bridesmaid. I said yes with a heart and a half. She joked that Dan calls me her 'other half', we spend so much time together. The date was set for August 2017.

I wasn't feeling well at their engagement drinks in December 2016 but didn't think much of it. Then I ended up in hospital in January and again in the February. Suddenly everything stopped as I was told the words you never think you're going to hear: 'It's cancer.'

I was hit with a hurricane of blood tests, MRIs and CTs. Words like 'chemo' and 'radiation' made me fall apart and the life that I knew stopped virtually overnight. Suddenly I was seeing an oncologist – how could this be happening? A few months ago I'd been dividing my time between work, the gym, yoga, the pub, nightclubs. Now I was either on the couch or in the hospital. I was planning my friend's hen from a chemo ward. This wasn't what we'd planned on those sun loungers.

I was admitted to hospital for all of April with an infection. Then my chemo schedule got moved around to the weekend of the hen. I obviously couldn't make it now. Everyone tried to involve me by sending me pictures and videos but it killed me to miss it.

In June they switched my chemo to a higher dose, along with radiation therapy. Treatment would take me right up to the week before the wedding. I was now unrecognisable. I'd lost stones in weight. My hair was almost gone, my skin was a mess. I had no energy and barely left my parents' house. I hated what my life had become. I tried to broach the subject of the wedding with Emma but she said she didn't care if I was there for an hour, a few hours, the day – whatever I wanted. We waited some more weeks. 'Let's see how you feel next week,' said everyone around me as we all tried not to think about what might happen.

Two weeks before the big day a decision had to be made: my mum did it for me, and said I was too ill to go. I was weirdly relieved it had been taken out of my hands but absolutely devastated I would miss her big day.

Mum rang Emma to tell her and they both cried. She called in and we both cried. Her mum called in and we cried. My other girlfriends heard I wouldn't make it, they rang or called in and we cried.

The day of the wedding came and I watched my best friend walk up the aisle on a webcam in my room. Thank god for technology, but this wasn't what I had planned. I cried as I watched them say their vows, watched them light candles, watched them promise to love each other. I cried as I knew I should be there standing next to her supporting her on the most important day of her life.

I hated what my life had become.

They mentioned me in the prayers of the faithful. They had my name on the order of service. They didn't replace me, I felt part of the day even though I didn't make it. In her speech she mentioned that she has two other halves, me and Dan, and everyone laughed as they toasted both of us. The girls sent me videos of the speeches as myself and my parents cried watching them in our sitting room.

Earlier that day she and Dan had called into my house on her way to the reception. She looked beautiful. She needed to use the toilet so I had to help her lift up her dress – we joked that I was doing my 'bridesmaid duty' by helping her to the toilet. I kept it together while they were in the house but the minute the door closed and they drove down the driveway I fell apart.

A picture of us together on that day is framed on my wall. It's a horrendous picture of me, I was so ill at the time but that's not important, the important thing is that Emma looked radiant and I got to see her on her big day.

When I look at that picture, I think of all our sun-lounger chats, all our plans and our hopes for the future. I think of where we thought we would be and what our lives would look like. I can't help but think of our innocence and how I had no idea of what was to come. I know that this is not the picture either of us imagined.

It was not the day I imagined.

This is not the life I imagined.

But I'm alive.

Triskele

Catherine Ann Cullen

I arabesque from the margins
of your great books.
You have not fathomed me.

I am older than letters:
I ripple from the first stone that skimmed the sea,
turn in infinite circles towards you.

I am the sweep of a quill,
the flourish of a turning feather,
the wind ruffling a wing,

a seashell whorl in the border,
the antlers of a great elk,
a serpent's curled tongue.

I mark time:
sunrise at winter solstice,
fireworks at year's turn.

I am the petroglyph at the gateway,
the threshold of the passage grave,
the portal to elsewhere,

the tendril curling towards light eternal,
the dark roots of the cosmic tree,
her luminous branches.

On my three legs, I hop from Athens to Sicily to Man.
Call me Trinacria, An Thríbhís Mhór, Triskele,
Three in One, Trinity.

I am three stools for milking a sacred cow,
three seats for a fireside of stories,
three tops spun on the hearth.

Find me in the minaret of Samarra,
on the endpapers of the Koran,
in the comb of the crowing cock.

I whirl in the spill of Hokusai waves,
in a Van Gogh skyscape,
on a Klimt dress.

I am without corners.
I say *Turn, turn again,*
change, remain.

Summer Snow

Susan Knight

A winding lane. On either side explosions of cow parsley, or Queen Anne's lace, which Sarah had always considered a more fitting name, given the intricate delicacy of the white flower heads. So narrow a lane that passing cars brushed between the bushes, but cars were blessedly rare.

It was Sarah's first time to wander here, lured out by the sun. She was renting a cottage in the valley for a couple of weeks, to draw and paint in peaceful isolation. After all the years, she still felt pretentious calling herself an artist, although that was how she supplemented her pension these days, selling her work in street markets or to friends and friends of friends.

With the delight of the city dweller when the countryside shows itself so lovely, she exclaimed at the surrounding mountains, their sinuous curves like reclining nudes. Hawthorns weighed down with May blossom. The startlingly yellow gorse that perfumed the air with coconut. Stone walls rusty with lichen or cushiony with moss. The babble of a mountain stream down the ditches. She examined every wild flower as she passed, wishing she knew its name. Of course, she recognised the buttercups that turned the meadows gold on either side. But in the hedgerows, tiny bursts of blue and pink and purple and yellow and white. After a while, although she hated picking flowers that so soon would die as a result – but there was so much, such profusion – she started to collect samples, to check out later.

Only the previous week she had visited an exhibition of botanical art with a friend who had oohed and aahed over the precise rendition of every curve of a petal or leaf, each frond of a fern, each baroque twist of a root. Each watercolour so precise, so detailed that the artists must have used the finest of sable brushes.

'You could do that,' her friend had remarked.

But she couldn't, or wouldn't even want to. Though undoubtedly skilled, there was something of the scientific specimen about these images, descendants of those made, before the invention of the camera, by artists accompanying expeditions to new worlds for the very purpose of recording exotic species. Her own style in oils and oil pastels was different, great slabs of colour and plenty of the ivory black that was a no-no with art teachers. Passionate pieces. Expressionist, she supposed, if her work had to be labelled.

Yes – picking a tiny yellow sprig – she would google them, for it was important to name things precisely. She had even heard there was an app you could download on to your smartphone that would identify any plant in the world if you took a picture of it. Progress, she supposed, everything becoming instantly accessible. Only she couldn't be bothered with apps and things like that. Not at her age.

Her age ... Sarah was still astonished to find that she had turned seventy. Seventy plus, actually. Whenever had that happened? When she was young, seventy-year-olds had seemed like dinosaurs, but now that she had crossed that particular Rubicon, she felt as young as ever, apart from all those aches and twinges, and the need to take a rest most afternoons. Not today, though. Today was so tempting, so golden, she had laid aside her brushes and put on her walking shoes.

The lane swayed round a bend and suddenly she gasped in delight, finding herself in the middle of a snowstorm. At least, that was how it seemed. A mass of tiny fluffy seed heads from some tree above her were being blown down by the warm breeze. She ambled through them and then looked back, only to find they had disappeared, like a dream, like magic. Wherever had they gone so suddenly? She retraced her steps and the storm of seeds reappeared. The sun, she realised, had illuminated them as she walked towards it. An enchantment of the light.

And suddenly Sarah remembered the first ever time she had seen summer snow. Long ago, in St Petersburg, as it now was, Leningrad as it was then. When Brezhnev's oppressive fist lay over the USSR.

She continued her walk, remembering. Dmitri, Dima. She had first got to know him on that student exchange programme. He wasn't handsome – not at all, being small and chubby – but he could make her laugh and she fell in love. She was twenty-two and dancing to 'Moonshadow' and 'American Pie' with the Marines at the American consulate. But they were nothing to her and she would run, the next morning, to meet Dima for breakfast in a canteen that served greasy blinis with sour cream and gave you your change in wrapped sweets. Once he had described his idea to set up such an establishment in the West, with fat and slovenly old women in grey socks sloshing filthy mops over the floor, wiping down Formica tables in front of you with wet rags, serving cutlets of an unidentifiable meat and soup bubbling with great lumps of fat.

'The Soviet culinary experience,' he'd said, laughing. 'I think I would make a fortune. Don't you agree?'

After breakfast they would go back to his shared room in a communal apartment. She would creep down the hall, not saying a word if they met anyone, so that spying neighbours wouldn't suspect she was a foreigner. Then they would make love. One time, he lifted her naked onto the table, under a lampshade shimmering with coloured beads. When she got up afterwards, the *Pravda* she had been lying on had transferred newsprint onto her bottom.

It wasn't on that first visit she had seen the summer snow, for it was autumn and then winter, the Neva frozen over and tough old men digging holes in the ice, stripping off and jumping in for just a few seconds. But she had returned the following summer to see

Dima again, and they had taken a walk by the little Fontanka river (that another Russian friend years later said resembled the Liffey – only with lots of good will and imagination, she thought). Hand in hand, they had wandered through the Admiralty Gardens and suddenly they were in a snowstorm. Great balls of fluffy seed heads falling around them, piling up on the paths and at the feet of the statue of Hercules. They had sat on a bench by the fountain.

'If you want to go to the West,' she had said to him, 'I will marry you.'

In those days the only way for Russian citizens to leave the Soviet Union was if they could prove they had even the tiniest drop of Jewish blood or if they married a westerner. Marriage was also used inside the country to acquire a permit to stay in the big cities. If Dima subsequently hadn't married his friend, Masha, on completion of his studies, he would have had to return to the provincial town where he was born. Such unions even had a name: fictitious marriages.

That day in the park, Dima had replied to her offer with a smile. 'Thank you,' he had said. 'It is so sweet of you. But, Sarah, what would I do in the West? I can't speak any language apart from Russian.'

'You could open a restaurant,' she had replied, and smiled too. But she was sad because she knew it was the end for them.

Around them the summer snow was still falling.

*

Sheep shorn to the skin stared at her with empty eyes. A white horse in a field paused in its chomping to give a high whinny. A small dog, tied up in a yard, barked suddenly, its impotent ferocity sounding out for a long time after she had passed. A monstrously huge truck carrying farm machinery approached, filling the lane so that she almost had to jump into the ditch not to be flattened. The driver raised his hand and she raised hers back. That, she had found, was the custom in the countryside, to acknowledge every driver, every passer-by. If you tried that in Dublin, she chuckled to herself, people would think you were mad.

Lilac was hanging over a cottage wall. Fat clusters of tiny mauve flowers. She buried her face in them and suddenly was a child again, inhaling the strong sweetness from the lilac tree in her parents' garden, comfort in the scent. But the mountains were turning black and gold as the sun sank lower. A mist was starting to rise from the fields. Sarah turned back.

*

Later that evening, a glass of wine beside her – a Douro from Portugal, fruity and not too heavy – and Miles Davis's 'Kind of Blue' on CD, she opened her laptop and started to google wild flowers of Ireland, identifying each of her collected specimens, and noting each one down because she knew too well that, at her age, it was difficult to remember such details, even though the names were so evocative. Cuckooflower, campion, bush vetch, mouse-ear, bird's-foot trefoil, cranesbill, columbine, forget-me-not ...

The task satisfactorily completed, she turned to Facebook. Jenny, she saw, wanted to save the orangutans, Bernadette proudly displayed pictures of her latest and frankly ugly grandchild, Michael was going to a protest meeting about the proposal to cut down trees in Fairview Park and invited everyone along, Rosie had run a marathon for a breast cancer charity and thanked her sponsors, James put up pictures of his Shih Tzu, Star, looking cute, Chuck something, a member of the US military, wanted to be her friend. Perhaps he was the son of one of the marines she had met all those years ago. The grandson, even. She deleted him, sipped her wine and turned off Facebook.

And then, as she sometimes did, she started to google old friends in case they had done something significant enough to pop up.

Dima had. He had died. She stared at the screen. *Our dear friend ... long illness ... to Germany for treatment ... thoughts are with Bella and Sveta ... the prime minister of Russia regrets ...* For, after all, Dima had become somebody, a famous economist. He had divorced Masha and married Bella, and Sarah had married dear Robbie, but they had kept in touch over the years and, like the civilised people they were, Robbie and Sarah had even visited Dima and Bella in Moscow a couple of times. But Robbie was long dead and now Dima was dead too.

She hadn't even known he was ill. As so often happens, and especially given the awkwardness of communicating with Russia, they had stopped writing for, oh, perhaps two, three, four years. More. Meaning to, but never getting around to it.

But why had his wife, his daughter, not told her? Did they think she wouldn't be interested?

Sarah poured herself another glass of wine. Yes, there was too much instant information, she decided. She could have bought a beautifully illustrated book on wildflowers. She could have left well alone and never googled old friends and lovers. That way she could have imagined they were living on somewhere, laughing, joking, crying, even. But still in this world. Not gone forever.

There is a poem by Michael Longley that has always moved her, about the killing of an ice-cream man in Belfast during the Troubles. Longley recites the names of the wildflowers of the Burren to soothe his young daughter's grief, with a reminder of the constancy and abundance of nature. Now Sarah took up her own list. She stood in the doorway of the cottage and looked up at the night sky, a full moon caught in black branches, and she started chanting in a low voice: cuckooflower, campion, bush vetch, mouse-ear, bird's-foot trefoil, cranesbill, columbine, forget-me-not ... cuckooflower, campion, bush vetch, mouse-ear, bird's-foot trefoil, cranesbill, forget-me-not ... cuckooflower, campion, bush vetch, mouse-ear, bird's-foot trefoil, cranesbill, forget-me-not ...

Vixen

Paul Bregazzi

Crossing the field of memory
between two shambolic stone
walls, a fox traverses a rushy field
sloughing off the Clare mist.
There she is.
Sopping, in wet-point,
prints a dancer's toe
in the slurried muck.
Benign –
on her own coney-quest, unknowing
of glass or scope or eye or thought –
just blacknail and raintrack,
mask, tippet and brush.

Fox

Mark Flynn

The thin, floppy-haired boy looked down at the book and back up again. That is definitely a fox, he said to himself, double-checking the illustrated pages in his lap. The late August evening, drained of its heat, smelled like summer's end. For the guts of an hour he had stuck it out in the grassy laneway, but it had been worth it. An actual red fox right here in front of him!

Staying as still as he could, David watched the fox slink along the line of hedgerow and disappear into the gap under a low-growing hawthorn tree. Behind him, the row of houses sat quiet and watchful in the gathering dusk. Of course, he knew what a fox looked like from television and books, but he'd never seen one in real life. This particular book had belonged to his mother and its illustrations showed a slightly different creature to the one he'd just seen. Book fox was a soft, fluffy and regal animal. Real fox looked a bit rougher around the edges, ragged and tough, but still, the coolest thing David had ever seen. He really loved the book and the notes his mother had made in the margins reminded him of her. He could still hear her voice in his mind, although the preciseness of tone and its character had been getting fainter as the months had passed. He imagined her whispering the fox-secret Latin she'd inscribed along the edge, *Vulpes vulpes noctis umbra*, as he waited for the animal to reappear.

*

The fox didn't come back through the gap, even though David waited a good twenty minutes. When you're nine years old, twenty minutes seems like an eternity and the bench was starting to hurt. To help pass the time David rummaged in his little backpack for something he could snack on. He had a half-full bottle of water and some chewy sweets. He appreciated the fact that they would take ages to eat and it was exactly what he needed to pass the time while waiting for another glimpse of the fox.

*

The shadows lengthened. Rival blackbirds rattled off silvery cannonades from opposing towers and David sat on the bench chewing his sweets. *Patience*, said his mother's neat marginalia, although it was in respect to sea otters and not foxes. However, the boy understood the sentiment to be the same. He thought about how he should have patience with his father and their new house in this strange county. Here, after all, they only had each other.

A wood pigeon battered its way through the ivy and launched itself over his head, clapping its wings for luck. The fox must know another way out, thought the boy, but he couldn't be sure, so he decided to wait a little more. The stars appeared overhead, twinkling into existence. David cradled the book and imagined his mother's voice letting him in on the secrets of the world. His father would soon be calling him home.

About the Writers

Anne Tannam has published three poetry collections: *Take This Life* (Wordonthestreet, 2011), *Tides Shifting Across my Sitting Room Floor* (Salmon Poetry, 2017) and *Twenty-six Letters of a New Alphabet* (Salmon Poetry, 2020).

Anne Marie Byrne has recently retired and is enjoying a life of leisure in her hometown of Bray. She welcomes the opportunity to contribute her first piece of creative writing to this anthology in support of Purple House, who provide invaluable support services to those affected by cancer.

Adam Wyeth is an award-winning writer and recipient of the 2019 Kavanagh Fellowship Award. He is the author of two poetry collections, *Silent Music* and *The Art of Dying*, and essays, *The Hidden World of Poetry*. His third collection, *about:blank*, will be published in 2020. He teaches online creative writing at adamwyeth.com.

David Butler's third novel, *City of Dis* (New Island), was short-listed for the Kerry Group Irish Novel of the Year 2015. Doire Press published his second poetry collection, *All the Barbaric Glass*, in 2017. His second short story collection, *Fugitive*, is forthcoming from Arlen House.

Edward O'Dwyer is the author of three collections of poems from Salmon Poetry: *The Rain on Cruise's Street* (2014), *Bad News,*

Good News, Bad News (2017) and *Exquisite Prisons* (2020). A collection of stories, *Cheat Sheets*, was published by Truth Serum Press in 2018. He lives in Limerick.

Rosemary Jenkinson was born in Belfast and is a playwright, short story writer and essayist. She was writer-in-residence at the Lyric Theatre and 2019 Arts Council of Northern Ireland Major Artist. Her latest short story collection is *Lifestyle Choice 10mg*, published by Doire Press.

Jean O'Brien's *Fish On A Bicycle: New & Selected Poems* was published by Salmon Poetry (2016). She won the Arvon and Fish International competition and was placed and highly commended in others including the Forward Prize. She is a recipient of a Kavanagh fellowship and holds an MPhil in Creative Writing and Poetry from Trinity College Dublin.

Neil Hegarty grew up in Derry. His novels include *The Jewel*, published to widespread praise in 2019; and *Inch Levels*, which was shortlisted for the Kerry Group Novel of the Year award in 2017. Neil's non-fiction titles include *The Story of Ireland*, which accompanies the BBC television history of Ireland.

Maria McManus was born in Enniskillen. She is the author of *Available Light* (Arlen House), *We Are Bone, The Cello Suites* and *Reading the Dog* (Lagan Press). Recent work includes poetry for the dance theatre productions *Dust* and *Turf* and the libretto for *Wretches: Revolutions, Rights & Wrongs*. She is artistic director of Poetry Jukebox.

Nuala O'Connor lives in Co. Galway. Her fourth novel, *Becoming Belle*, was recently published to critical acclaim in the US, Ireland and the UK. Her forthcoming novel is about Nora Barnacle, wife and muse to James Joyce. Nuala is editor at flash e-zine *Splonk*.

Geraldine O'Kane is a poet, creative writing facilitator and mental health advocate. She gave a talk for TEDx Belfast in 2015 on how creativity helps mental health. She is a recipient of the Artist Career Enhancement Scheme (ACES) from the Arts Council of Northern Ireland. Her collection is due late 2020 from Salmon Poetry.

Mia Gallagher writes novels, stories and non-fiction and has devised and written for the stage. Her critically acclaimed books include the novels *HellFire* and *Beautiful Pictures of the Lost Homeland* and a short story collection, *Shift*. Mia is a contributing editor with *The Stinging Fly* and a member of Aosdána.

Winner of the Trocaire/Poetry Ireland and Poems for Patience competitions, **Maurice Devitt** has been nominated for Pushcart, Forward and Best of the Net prizes and been runner-up in the Cúirt New Writing Prize, Interpreter's House Poetry Competition and the Cork Literary Review Manuscript Competition. He published his debut collection, *Growing Up in Colour*, with Doire Press.

John O'Donnell's fiction and poetry has been published and broadcast widely in Ireland and abroad. Awards include the Irish National Poetry Prize, the Ireland Funds Prize and Hennessy Awards for Poetry and Fiction. He is the author of four poetry collections and a collection of short stories, *Almost the Same Blue* (Doire Press, 2020).

Brian Kirk is a poet and writer from Dublin. He published a poetry collection, *After the Fall* (Salmon Poetry, 2017), and a fiction chapbook, *It's Not Me, It's You* (Southword Editions, 2019). His poem 'Birthday' was chosen as Irish Poem of the Year at the Irish Book Awards in 2018.

Niamh Boyce was awarded New Irish Writer of the Year 2012 for her poetry. Her bestselling debut, *The Herbalist* (2013), was an Irish

Book Awards winner and longlisted for the 2015 IMPAC award. Her latest book, *Her Kind* (2019), was based on the Kilkenny witchcraft trial and nominated for the EU Prize for Literature.

Stephanie Conn's debut collection, *The Woman on the Other Side* (Doire Press), and her pamphlet 'Copeland's Daughter' (Smith/Doorstop) were published in 2016. *Island* (Doire Press) was published in 2018. She is currently working on a new collection, while dealing with chronic illness, as part of a PhD by Practice at Ulster University.

Danielle McLaughlin's short story collection *Dinosaurs on Other Planets* was published in 2015 by The Stinging Fly Press. She was a 2019 Windham-Campbell Prize recipient and won the *Sunday Times* Audible Short Story Award. Her first novel, *The Art of Falling*, will be published in 2021.

Katie Donovan has published five collections of poetry, all with Bloodaxe Books. Her first collection, *Watermelon Man*, appeared in 1993, followed by *Entering the Mare, Day of the Dead* and *Rootling: New and Selected Poems*. Her most recent collection, *Off Duty*, was shortlisted for the 2017 Poetry Now Award. She is a recipient of the Lawrence O'Shaughnessy Award for Irish Poetry.

Veronica O'Leary is the founder and director of services at Purple House Cancer Support. She lives in Bray, Co. Wicklow, with her husband Brendan. They have two sons, Ronan and Conor. In her downtime Veronica enjoys walking in the mountains, singing, planting veg and tending her garden.

Arnold Thomas Fanning's work has been published in *The Dublin Review, Banshee, gorse, The Lonely Crowd, The Stinging Fly, Correspondences: An Anthology to Call for an End to Direct Provision* and elsewhere. *Mind on Fire: A Memoir of Madness and Recovery* (Penguin Ireland, 2018) was shortlisted for the 2019 Wellcome Book Prize.

Nessa O'Mahony is from Dublin. She has published five books of poetry, the most recent being *The Hollow Woman on the Island* (Salmon Poetry, 2019). Her crime novel, *The Branchman*, was published by Arlen House in 2018.

Catherine Dunne's novels have been shortlisted for Kerry Group Novel of the Year, Listowel, the Irish Book Awards, the International Strega Prize and longlisted for the International Dublin Literary Award. She won the Giovanni Boccaccio International Prize for Fiction in 2013. She was the 2018 recipient of the Irish PEN Award for Literature.

Jessica Traynor is an award-winning poet, creative writing teacher and librettist from Dublin. Books include *Liffey Swim* (2014) and *The Quick* (2018), both published by Dedalus Press. Her opera, *Paper Boat*, commissioned by Music for Galway and co-produced with Irish National Opera, will be performed in 2021.

Eamon McGuinness's fiction has appeared in *The Stinging Fly* and *Crannóg*. He was the winner of the Michael McLaverty and Wild Atlantic Words short story competitions in 2019. He holds an MA in Creative Writing from UCD. His debut poetry collection is forthcoming from Salmon Poetry.

Noel Duffy's debut collection, *In the Library of Lost Objects* (Ward Wood Publishing, 2012), was shortlisted for the Shine/Strong Award for best first collection by an Irish poet. His second collection, *On Light & Carbon*, followed in autumn 2013, with a third, *Summer Rain*, appearing in 2016. His most recent collection, *Street Light Amber*, was published in spring 2020.

Alan McMonagle has written for radio and published two collections of short stories. *Ithaca*, his first novel, was published by Picador in 2017 as part of a two-book deal. His second novel,

Laura Cassidy's Walk of Fame, was published in March 2020. He lives in Galway.

Paul Perry is the author of five full-length collections of poetry including *Gunpowder Valentine* (Dedalus, 2014). He is Head of Creative Writing at UCD. His new novel, *The Garden*, is forthcoming from New Island Books.

Roisín O'Donnell won the Irish Book Awards Short Story of the Year 2018. Her debut story collection, *Wild Quiet*, was published in 2016. Her stories have appeared in *The Stinging Fly*, *The Irish Times* and elsewhere, and feature in the landmark anthologies *The Long Gaze Back* and *The Glass Shore*.

Kate Dempsey's poetry is published in Ireland and the UK. She won the Plough Prize and has been shortlisted for the Hennessy New Irish Writing Award. Her debut collection, *The Space Between*, was published by Doire Press in 2016. She runs the Poetry Divas, a glittery collective of women poets who blur the wobbly boundary between page and stage.

Madeleine D'Arcy's short story collection, *Waiting for the Bullet* (Doire Press, 2014), won the Edge Hill Readers' Choice Prize 2015. She received Hennessy New Irish Writing and First Fiction awards in 2010. Her second collection will be published in 2021. She has recently completed a novel.

Colin Dardis is a poet, editor, sound artist and arts coordinator from Northern Ireland. His collections include *The Dogs of Humanity* (Fly on the Wall Press, 2019) and *the x of y* (Eyewear, 2018). His work has been published widely throughout Ireland, the UK and the US.

Mary Morrissy is the author of three novels, *Mother of Pearl*, *The Pretender* and *The Rising of Bella Casey* and two collections of stories, *A Lazy Eye* and most recently, *Prosperity Drive*. She is Associate Director of Creative Writing at University College Cork and a member of Aosdána.

Mary O'Donnell's seven poetry collections include *Unlegendary Heroes* and *Those April Fevers*. Her four novels include *Where They Lie* and the bestselling debut *The Light Makers,* reissued in 2017 by 451 Editions. In 2018 Arlen House published her short story collection, *Empire. Massacre of the Birds*, a new anthology, is forthcoming from Salmon Poetry. She is a member of Aosdána.

Novelist **Emma Hannigan** was born in Bray in 1971. A carrier of the breast cancer gene BRCA1, she survived cancer eleven times, was ambassador for Breast Cancer Ireland, raised €1.4 million for cancer research and sold half a million copies of her novels. Emma died on 3 March 2018. Her loss is irreplaceable.

Inspired by myth and nature, **Breda Wall Ryan'**s poetry has won multiple awards, including the Gregory O'Donoghue International Poetry Prize and the Dermot Healy International Poetry Award. Her first collection, *In a Hare's Eye* (Doire Press, 2015), won the Shine/Strong Award. *Raven Mothers* (Doire Press, 2018) is her second collection. She lives in Bray.

Órla Foyle's first novel, *Belios*, was published by The Lilliput Press in 2005. Her poetry collection, *Red Riding Hood's Dilemma* (2010), was published by Arlen House, as was her short fiction, *Somewhere in Minnesota* (2011) and *Clemency Browne Dreams of Gin* (2014). Her work has been published in *The Dublin Review, The Stinging Fly, The Manchester Review, The Wales Arts Review* and *gorse*.

Emma McKervey lives in Ballywalter, Co. Down. She recently collaborated with her husband, artist Philip Mussen, on an exhibition, Beneath the Mantle, exploring Neolithic and early Christian sites on the Ards peninsula. Her book *The Rag Tree Speaks* (2017) is published by Doire Press.

Geraldine Mills is the author of three collections of short fiction, a children's novel and five collections of poetry, the most recent being *Bone Road* (Arlen House, 2019). Her awards include a Hennessy/*Sunday Tribune* New Irish Award, a Patrick and Katherine Kavanagh Fellowship and two Arts Council bursaries.

Eleanor Hooker's third poetry collection is forthcoming. Her poems have been published in journals including *Poetry Ireland Review*, *Poetry* magazine, *Winter Papers*, *PN Review* and *Agenda*. Eleanor is a helm on the Lough Derg RNLI lifeboat. She began her career as a nurse and midwife.

Lisa Harding's latest novel, *Bright Burning Things*, will be published by Bloomsbury in March 2021. Her first novel, *Harvesting* (New Island, 2018), was shortlisted for the Kerry Group Prize. Lisa was voted best newcomer at the Irish Book Awards and won the Kate O'Brien award in 2018.

Ferdia Mac Anna was born in Dublin and works as a novelist, film director, screenwriter and lecturer. He produced a BAFTA-winning BBC/RTÉ drama series, *Custer's Last Stand-Up*. In 1996 his novel, *The Last of the High Kings*, was made into a Hollywood movie. He has directed short films, documentaries and TV dramas as well as the feature films *All About Eva* (2015) and *DannyBoy* (2019).

Ann Hickey is married to Michael and lives in Glenageary, Co. Dublin. She has two adult sons and has reason to be very grateful to Purple House as fourteen years ago she was diagnosed with breast cancer. Purple House was, and still is, her lifeline.

Eithne Lannon is a poet from Dublin. Her writing has been published in various contemporary literary journals and anthologies. She has been shortlisted for a number of competitions including the 2020 Shine/Strong Poetry Award. Eithne's first collection, *Earth Music*, was published in 2019 by Turas Press.

Niall McArdle's work has appeared in *The Irish Times*, *Banshee*, *Spontaneity*, the *RTÉ Guide*, AGNI Online and *Phoenix Irish Short Stories* 2003 and has been broadcast on RTÉ Radio. In 2018 he was the winner of the RTÉ Guide/Penguin Ireland Short Story Competition, and he has been shortlisted for the Hennessy Literary Awards, the Francis MacManus Short Story Competition and the Cúirt New Writing Prize. He lives in Dublin.

Brendan O'Leary's literary career began at the age of twelve when he won a school essay competition: the prize was a Kodak camera presented by the Lord Mayor of Dublin. Winning the competition was a big deal and his proud parents were probably as amazed as he was. He fell in love with that plastic Kodak camera and so began a lifelong interest in photography.

Rachel Blayney would never have given writing a go but for Purple House. She had an adventurous childhood, always surrounded by animals. She studied nursing in Dublin and kept her keen interest in observing and communicating: now with cancer yet still the adventurer.

Phil Lynch's poems have appeared in various literary journals and anthologies. He is a regular reader and performer of his work at events in Ireland and abroad. His collection, *In a Changing Light*, was published in 2016 by Salmon Poetry.

Katie Boylan has been a member of the Purple House Creative Writing Group since it started. She lives in Dublin with her two sound housemates, who also happen to be her parents, Basher and Trishie. She studied film in college but ended up working in advertising to pay the bills. She enjoys reading, cinema, red wine, yoga and chocolate; but her real love is her black Labrador, Rocky.

Catherine Ann Cullen is the inaugural poet in residence at Poetry Ireland. She is an award-winning poet, children's writer and songwriter. She has published three collections, including *The Other Now* (Dedalus, 2016) and three children's books, including *All Better!* (Little Island, 2019). She has a PhD in Creative Writing from Middlesex University.

Susan Knight has written three novels and three collections of short stories, including *Out of Order* (Arlen House, 2015) and *Mrs Hudson Investigates* (MX publishing, 2019). Her ten-minute play, *Mistaken*, was produced in 2019 as part of Dublin's Short & Sweet festival. She teaches creative writing at the People's College.

Paul Bregazzi's poetry has appeared in *The Irish Times*, *Poetry Ireland Review*, *Crannóg* and *Magma* amongst others. He was selected for Poetry Ireland's Introductions Series 2015 and was winner of Cúirt New Writing Prize for Poetry 2017. His debut collection, *Hex*, is forthcoming from Salmon Poetry.

Mark Flynn is an award-winning musician from Darndale on Dublin's northside. As well as singing, fishing and foraging, he is also writing a children's novel and a collection of darkly honest short stories. His flash-fiction piece, 'Fox', was a prizewinner in the 2019 Bray Literary Festival flash-fiction competition.